The Experience Club

The Rediscovered Cases of Sherlock Holmes Book 7

Arthur Hall

Paperback 978-1-78705-982-5
ePub ISBN 978-1-78705-983-2
PDF ISBN 978-1-78705-984-9

MX Publishing
335 Princess Park Manor, Royal Drive,
London, N11 3GX
www.mxpublishing.com

Cover design by Brian Belanger
www.belangerbooks.com and www.redbubble.com/people/zhahadun

Arthur Hall was born in Aston, Birmingham, UK, in 1944. His interest in writing began during his schooldays and served as a growing ambition to become an author.

Years later, his first novel 'Sole Contact' was an espionage story about an ultra-secret government department known as 'Sector Three' and has been followed, to date, by five sequels.

Other works include seven 'rediscovered' cases from the files of Sherlock Holmes, two collections of short stories featuring The Great Detective, two collections of bizarre tales and two novels about an adventurer called 'Bernard Kramer', as well as several contributions to the ongoing anthology, 'The MX Book of New Sherlock Holmes Stories'.

His only ambition, apart from being published more widely, is to attend the premier of a film based on one of his novels, ideally at The Odeon, Leicester Square.

He lives in the West Midlands, United Kingdom, where he often walks other people's dogs as he attempts to formulate new plots.

Details of his work can be seen at:

arthurhallsbooksite.blogspot.com, and the author can be contacted at: arthurhall7777@aol.co.uk

By the same author:

CONTENTS

Chapter 1 – A Request for Assistance

Holmes and I climbed the stairs to our Baker Street rooms wearily. My friend appeared untroubled by the cross-examination of counsel for the prosecution which he had endured less than two hours ago, for he had emerged victorious. This was the culmination of a long-expected summons to court and he had relished it, for he had always held that Fergus Stone was entirely innocent of the monstrous double-kidnapping charge that Scotland Yard had attributed to him.

"You can be proud of yourself this day, Holmes," I remarked. "It is no small thing to restore the liberty of an innocent man, against such odds."

"It is true that Sir Silas Crowther is a formidable opponent, but the facts, presented in the correct order, revealed the undeniable truth. When I pointed out the shortcomings in Inspector Trevalyn's investigation, and they were acknowledged, I knew that Mr Stone would leave the court a free man." He hung up his hat and coat and smiled. "But now the time for luncheon approaches, and I believe I hear Mrs Hudson on the stairs already. Let us take our places at the table, Watson, and await whatever delights she has prepared for us."

After the ordeal of the morning, at least for me, we were glad to enjoy a rich beef stew. I was glad to see Holmes consume his food with an unusual relish, although he refused the following treacle tart and custard in favour of several cups of strong coffee. I pushed away my dessert plate and filled my cup with the steaming liquid, feeling pleasantly satisfied.

"What do you propose for this afternoon, Holmes?" I asked.

He shrugged. "I have several chemical experiments awaiting completion, but I think some attention to my index must come first. As you know, it has been most useful on occasion, and the demands on my time of late have caused me to neglect its upkeep."

"The same is true of the accumulating pile of medical journals that seem to be arriving with increasing frequency. I really cannot afford to leave them any longer."

"Then it is settled." He sprang from his chair, still full of the nervous energy that is his driving force. "We shall experience a quiet, but enlightening, afternoon."

But the prospect was short-lived. I rose from the table and looked down on Baker Street from our half-open window, knowing at once that our plans were about to be shattered.

"It is likely that our intentions will be altered, Holmes."

He looked up from the volume he had selected. "Why should that be, old fellow?"

"Because there is a young man in rather an alarming condition, approaching the front door with difficulty."

Holmes replaced the scrapbook, stood beside me and glanced down without comment.

The door-bell rang and we waited in silence. Moments later Mrs Hudson announced a tall, upright man who I judged to be about thirty-five and had clearly suffered some injury, before hurriedly clearing away the remains of our meal. Our visitor appeared rather taken aback, obviously uncertain as to which of us to address.

"I am Sherlock Holmes," my friend volunteered. "This is my associate, Doctor John Watson. Whatever your problem may be sir, be assured that you can speak as freely before him as to me."

"Thank you, gentlemen. I am most grateful to you for admitting me without an appointment."

"I see that you have recently endured some distress," Holmes continued. "Will you take a glass of brandy to calm your nerves?"

"No, thank you Mr Holmes, for I have come to realise that I must recover myself without the aid of artificial stimulants."

"Coffee then, or tea?"

He shook his head, and the cuts on his face glittered with congealed blood. "The truth is, I have hardly given any thought to food and drink of late."

"Take the basket chair then, and tell us how we can help you. We are at your disposal."

At my invitation he removed his hat and coat, and we all sat before the unlit fire. "I know that you keep abreast of things Mr Holmes, so you will have heard of the three murders of last week."

"The dailies have featured them prominently, and there was some talk of growing panic. I recall that a woman was stabbed to death in a railway carriage, a man poisoned in a restaurant and some fellow shot through the heart in his club."

"Indeed. The panic came about because it was assumed that the killings were connected, and rumours of a wanton murderer stalking the streets of London in search of victims prevailed. The sensationalist press has much to answer for."

"Then there is, in fact, no such possibility?"

"I suspect a connection but cannot say with certainty, for I am not far into the case."

Holmes gave him a curious look. "Are you connected with Scotland Yard? I observed you approaching our front door and recognised your movements as resembling a march rather than a stride. It follows therefore, that you have been associated with either the military or the police."

"Not any more, sir. I was forced by circumstance to abandon my position. Since then I have adopted the same employment as yourself."

"You are a consulting detective?" I ventured with some surprise.

"I functioned more as an enquiry agent, which is how I was reduced to the state in which you now see me."

"It would be best, I think, if you were to tell us your tale from the beginning," Holmes said after a moment. "Pray endeavour to include all details."

Our client was silent, probably collecting his thoughts, for as long as it took him to inhale deeply. Then, after a nervous glance at each of us, he explained the purpose of his visit.

"My name is Josiah Endicott," he began. "Your observation was quite correct, Mr Holmes, for many are the times I have marched with a party of constables in the course of my duty with the Northumberland Division of the official force. About a year ago, having reached the rank of sergeant, I was about to seek further promotion with the plain-clothes branch, when I had to give up my post to nurse my wife as she slowly succumbed to consumption."

Holmes and I expressed our condolences.

"Thank you, gentlemen," our visitor continued. "After Gwendolyn passed on I existed in a dazed state for a time, until I realised that I must resume earning my living before I became impoverished. All I had ever known was Northumberland and the law, so I resolved to make a fresh start. I would journey to the capital and make my future there. I considered seeking a position at Scotland Yard, but hesitated at the thought of how the application of a former Northumberland sergeant might be received. Also I felt an unfamiliar desire to work alone, to see what could be accomplished."

Holmes leaned his thin form forward in his chair. "And so, you began a new career as an enquiry agent."

"That is how it was. This was six months ago, and I have since enjoyed some success at tracing people who, for one reason or another, have become estranged from their families or friends. I seemed to be making some headway in my chosen new direction, until I took it upon myself to study such details as the newspapers have published concerning the murders that I have already referred to."

"What, especially, attracted your attention to these?"

"One of the victims, Mr Seth Cornwell, was attached to the Detective Branch of Scotland Yard. Shortly before his retirement he had occasion to visit the station where I served in Northumberland, and I was able to assist him slightly in the enquiry which had brought him to us. We became friends, I suppose you could say, although it was very much like a father-and-son relationship, but he was tireless in his encouragement of my plans for advancement."

"So you decided to investigate his death, because of the intimacy that had existed between you."

"Indeed, sir. I read that he died while in the company of a young woman, Miss Daisy Scanlon, as they dined together in a local restaurant. The newspapers revealed that Inspector Gregson of Scotland Yard has interviewed her, and reported that she was suffering great distress. He found no reason to connect her with the killing. Nevertheless, it seemed the obvious place to start my own enquiries, so I called to see the lady at her home in Harrow. She admitted me reluctantly, saying that the police had already been there, and I learned little except that her anguish seemed entirely real. It was on my way back to the capital that my carriage was brought to a halt by the sight of a body lying in its path. This proved to be a ruse, as the injured man leapt to his feet and held the cabby at gunpoint as he went to help. At the same time I was dragged to the ground by two roughs who appeared from among the trees and proceeded to beat me until I became unconscious. My last blurred memory of that incident is of the cruel face that stared into my own, telling me that my life would be forfeit if I visited Miss Scanlon again, *or the others.*"

"I would be glad to examine your injuries, if you so wish," I offered.

For the first time, the ghost of a smile crept across his strained countenance. "Thank you, Doctor, but the cab driver delivered me to Saint Bartholomew's Hospital, after my assailants had run off. Beneath my clothes I am bandaged, and I have been prescribed a regular dose of laudanum until my recovery is complete."

"You have concluded then, that your attacker's remark reveals that all three murders of last week are connected?" Holmes enquired.

"It seemed to me to be worth investigating. I cannot see why it should not be so, because otherwise each crime appears pointless."

Holmes allowed his head to fall upon his chest, apparently deep in thought.

"Have you made this occurrence known to Scotland Yard?" he asked presently.

The cry of a newspaper-seller reached us through the half-open window, as our client adjusted his position painfully. "I approached Inspector Gregson, as he was previously involved in the enquiry into Mr Cornwell's murder, but he advised me only that his investigation was proceeding. He considered my experience to have no definite connection, as such incidents take place in and around the capital every day. The remark of my attacker, he said, could have a variety of meanings. I formed the opinion that my interference was resented."

"No doubt you are correct in that," Holmes allowed. "I had hoped the Scotland Yarders had learned to listen more closely to victims and witnesses over the years, but sometimes I wonder at their continued obtuseness. I assume, Mr Endicott, that you then sought to perpetuate your enquiry, by referring it to us?"

"I have followed your cases in the newspapers at length. You seemed the appropriate choice, after the official force showed such disinterest."

If my friend felt disappointment or outrage at the prospect of being considered second choice after Scotland Yard, he showed nothing of it. His sleepy demeanour was suddenly cast aside, and I saw that his eyes glittered at the prospect of a new case.

"Very well, Mr Endicott, you may go home and leave this with us. Watson and myself will do what we can. Be assured that we will get to the bottom of things, in one way or another. But first, if you will kindly furnish us with some details."

Mr Endicott produced several sheets of paper from a pocket of his coat. "I have committed it all to writing. These are, of course, my own private conclusions and observations. I hope they will be of some assistance to you."

"I am certain of it," Holmes said after accepting the sheets and running his eyes over the script quickly. "But now I see that you are in need of sleep and convalescence and, since you have described your findings so well, there is no need to detain you further. Be assured that you will hear from us before long."

With that we all rose. Our client thanked us with some embarrassment, and left us shortly afterwards. We heard the front door close behind him, before Holmes spoke.

"I thought better of Gregson."

"Possibly his attention has shifted to other things. The Millington train robbery and the rumours of forthcoming assassination attempts on members of the government, and even the royal family, must be occupying much of his time. Lestrade, as you know, is in Aberdeen."

"Quite so. How do you suggest that we proceed, Watson?"

"First, you will need to peruse those documents."

He nodded. "And I will do so, this evening. We may, however, be able to make a start this afternoon. May I take it that you are with me?"

"Of course. As soon as I have collected my service weapon."

"Since we do not know, as yet, the full nature of what we are about to embark upon, that would be as well. Clearly, the home of Miss Daisy Scanlon was under observation by our adversaries, whoever they may be, which also suggests that this affair was planned in advance."

"Where, then, do we begin?" I felt the peaceful few hours that I had expected suddenly slip away. Already, Holmes' movements had become like those of a foxhound, restrained but ready to begin the chase.

He glanced at the papers again. "Mr Endicott has compiled these details well. Mr Seth Cornwell, was poisoned while enjoying a meal in the Carousel Restaurant in Harrow. There is time, I think, for us to visit Miss Scanlon, even at the cost of our dinner suffering some delay."

With that we retrieved our hats and coats. We stood in the late spring sunshine for several minutes, before a hansom deposited a fare nearby. Holmes strode across the street with me in his wake, and we were comfortably settled as the frisky gelding set off along Baker Street at a fast pace.

Sometime later, we neared our destination as the trees leaning from both sides of the road gave way suddenly to a considerable number of houses, together with a church, a public house and a row of shops. As we passed I noticed that the Carousel Restaurant appeared to be a popular and well-turned out establishment, with a large blackboard outside on which today's menu was displayed. We paid off the hansom, and it had scarcely vanished from our sight when my friend raised his stick to indicate our destination.

"There is the house we seek, Watson. It is much as our client described it in his notes."

I had to agree that the writings had been comprehensive. The tiny cottage was one of a thatched-roofed group of four. I noted, as I knew that Holmes had, that all the curtains were drawn.

He rapped upon the door, and presently we heard slow footsteps from within. It opened, slowly at first, to reveal a fair-haired young girl in some distress. Tears flowed down her face, as she enquired as to our business.

"My name is Sherlock Holmes," he replied, "and this is my friend and colleague Doctor John Watson. We are continuing an investigation into the death of Mr Seth Cornwell, in whose company we believe you were at the time of his unfortunate demise. We would be grateful for a few minutes of your time to that end."

Miss Scanlon regarded us blankly for several moments, then she nodded with what appeared to be reservation and, still sobbing quietly, stood aside for us to enter.

We were led into a spotless room, decorated with tasteful wall-hangings and copper bed-warmers from a previous age. The furniture was well-polished and the carpet, I would have said, was of Turkish origin. Our hostess bade us sit and offered tea, which we refused.

"Please, gentlemen, ask your questions," she invited through a vale of tears.

"It is obvious that you are very upset," Holmes began in a softer tone, "so we will endeavour to bring this interview to a close as quickly as can be. Firstly, I would be grateful if you would enlighten us as to your connection with Mr Cornwell."

Miss Scanlon removed her handkerchief from her face. "He lived next door. Shortly after I came to live here, about a year ago, we began chatting over the garden fence and soon became friends. One day he and I chanced to be eating in the restaurant down the road at the same time, and soon began to attend there together regularly. He used to entertain me with stories of his years in the police, and after a while I learned that people around here had assumed that he was my grandfather."

"Then it is his death that has distressed you so," I said.

She nodded. "That, and my guilt."

"Kindly elaborate." Holmes requested curiously.

"There are things I could not bring myself to tell the police, when they came to investigate, or the kind gentleman who followed. Now, increasingly with each passing day, they weigh upon my conscience more heavily than I can bear."

"If you unburden yourself to us, we will do our utmost to help you, if that is at all possible."

She looked steadily at Holmes, then at me, before deciding to speak.

"I do not believe that anyone can save me," she said in a dull tone, "though I would welcome your assistance. Truly, I am desperate."

I felt pity for her. "Come now, in my experience there are not many situations that are absolutely hopeless."

"Here, I fear that it is so." She shook her head in anguish. "I am for the hangman."

Holmes and I glanced at each other, as the sound of a horse galloping by reached us from the road. It faded into the distance before he spoke.

"How can that be?" He asked softly.

She closed her eyes, as if her own words caused her agony. "Because it was I, who killed him."

Chapter Two – The Mysterious Doctor Andovene

There was silence in the room, except for the singing of birds in the garden.

"Pray begin at wherever you perceive the beginning of these events to be," Holmes requested. "Leaving out not the smallest detail."

She wiped away her tears with a saturated handkerchief, a picture of misery. "I see now that I have been duped but I did not, at first, understand the reason. I have been foolish, indeed." After a visible effort to contain herself, she told us all. "About two months ago I was shopping in London, when a robber snatched my purse. As he made off he was caught by a man who emerged from the crowd after apparently witnessing the incident. This stranger held the thief by the scruff of his neck and administered a hearty slap to his face, which made him fall to the pavement before running away. My saviour introduced himself as Doctor Andovene, of St Bart's Hospital, and returned my purse to me. About a week later we met again by chance, as I emerged from a greengrocer's shop that I often patronise. He invited me to a tea-room, where we had a long and companionable conversation. Presently he asked if he could call upon me, and I agreed. Almost before I realised it, I was being courted by this handsome newcomer to my life."

Holmes gave me a knowing glance. We had heard many similar tales over the years, but to this uncomplicated country girl it was a new experience.

"From that day then, you saw this man regularly?" he ventured.

"Once, sometimes twice every week. We enjoyed each other's company, and I grew to care for him."

"Did Mr Cornwell ever meet him?"

"No, but he saw him once from a distance, and made no comment. Doctor Andovene apparently knew him from before, however, and it did not surprise me that Mr Cornwell had no recollection of that, since he lately suffered from bouts of absent-mindedness."

"Did Doctor Andovene display a measure of familiarity with Mr Cornwell's past, since he claimed to be part of it."

Miss Scanlon had ceased to cry. She now reflected thoughtfully. "I believe so. He certainly was aware of Mr Cornwell's long employment with the police authorities. Also, he knew that Mr Cornwell had a life-long fear of drugs and the workings of the medical profession, accepting only herbal remedies for his infrequent ailments. Doctor Andovene mentioned that, some years ago, Mr Cornwell had refused a treatment for rheumatism that he had proposed."

"Did you mention this to Mr Cornwell?" I asked.

She nodded. "He remembered no such incident, nor ever attending a doctor's surgery. Doctor Andovene knew of the severe indigestion that had plagued Mr Cornwell for years though, and in the course of one of our conversations I confirmed to him that this had persisted."

"He suggested a remedy, of course?" Holmes enquired. Clearly, he had already understood the situation.

"He did, after expressing great sympathy for Mr Cornwell," Miss Scanlon looked faintly surprised at my friend's grasp of events, "Doctor Andovene gave me a twist of paper containing a white powder. Because of Mr Cornwell's aversion to drugs, he instructed me to add this to his food unbeknown to him. He assured me that this was a commonplace and harmless remedy that is widely used successfully, and I obeyed with the best of intentions." She was on the verge of a fresh flow of tears, but she fought them back bravely. "The result, gentlemen, you already know, and you will understand why I have not divulged the full story before. There can be no question that I was the instrument of Mr Cornwell's death, however unwittingly, and now I have lightened my burden of guilt by confessing it to you. I will accompany you if you wish, or I will await the arrival of the official force to take me into custody. I can do no more now, than accept my punishment for ending the life of a dear friend."

Silence hung heavily over us for a long moment. Holmes' expression had become flint-like and I could not have predicted his response. Miss Scanlon had adopted a certain resignation, as if the coldness of the condemned cell had already penetrated her bones.

"You have been cruelly used, and your affections trifled with," he said at last. "You may be certain of my intention to explain the true circumstances to the authorities, and of any further assistance that may be necessary. Miss Scanlon, your information has been invaluable to my investigation, and I thank you for it. I have one more question, to which I would be grateful for your answer."

I saw that relief had crept into her face. "I cannot sufficiently express my thanks, nor convey to you the anxiety you have dispelled. Pray tell me what it is that you wish to know."

"Only whether you attempted to find Doctor Andovene, when the true circumstances became apparent to you."

"I went into the capital for that purpose, although I did not as yet recognise the extent to which I had been deceived, the day after Mr Cornwell died. I discovered that Doctor Andovene was unknown at St Alwyn's Place, where he had claimed to reside, neither had anyone at St Bart's Hospital heard his name. I have never before felt so foolish and embarrassed."

"It is certain that this man, whoever he truly is, has falsely represented himself to you. Undoubtedly he has committed such deeds many times before. He is quite professional at his craft, and doubtlessly his victims are many. It follows that your only error was to misplace your trust, and that is understandable and certainly no crime. There is no reason for you to blame yourself."

"You are very kind and understanding."

Holmes rose and I did likewise. "But now we must leave you. Is it possible to visit Mr Cornwell's cottage, would you say?"

"No one has done so since the police made their examination. I do not know where a key can be found."

"That is a minor problem," Holmes smiled faintly. "We will see what can be done. My thanks, and do not allow anxiety to despoil your life, I beg of you. I will not forget my promise to put matters right."

With that we took our leave of her, and Holmes turned his attention to the cottage next door. His pick-lock gained us an easy entry and he spent some little time examining the rooms, until he finally turned away in disgust.

"The local police, and probably Scotland Yard, have stamped all over this place. We have wasted our time here, Watson."

After he had re-locked the door we set off along the tree-lined road, for there was no sign of a cab hereabouts. We walked briskly for about a mile before we encountered a land-worker who was on his way home in a cart. He took us on until we neared the outskirts of the capital, where we left him and procured a hansom that had just delivered a fare to a private house.

Mrs Hudson's chicken pie was most welcome after our exertions, and we repaired to our usual armchairs the moment the coffee pot was empty and the plates cleared away.

We lit our pipes and recounted the events of the day for a while, and then my friend returned to a more thorough scrutiny of Mr Josiah Endicott's notes while I once more perused my accumulated medical journals. At least half the evening had passed in this way when the door-bell rang loudly, stirring me from a contented doze.

I had feared that another case was about to confront Holmes, but Mrs Hudson brought to us not a client but a telegram. Holmes tore open the envelope with a thumbnail and read the contents briefly.

"It is from Miss Scanlon, Watson. She has discovered some new facts that she believes will interest us. We are to meet her at Resurrection Church Hall, near Hampstead Heath, at ten tomorrow morning."

I nodded. "What did you make of her, Holmes?"

"I saw no deception or guile in her," he said as he resumed his seat. "She appears to have lived an uncomplicated life, probably with few suitors, in rural Harrow. Her account of events however, tells us certain things about our adversaries. Both encounters with this Doctor Andovene were planned of course, and for some time ahead since he knew much about both Miss Scanlon and Mr Cornwell. I have no doubt that Mr Cornwell's failure to recollect their previous meeting was not due to absent-mindedness, but because it never occurred. This 'Doctor' is evidently a professional trickster of some sort, and an unsophisticated country girl such as Miss Scanlon must have been very easy prey. We have seen that he does not flinch at murder, and we do not yet know his purpose in killing Mr Cornwell, or whether he is responsible for the two other murders as our client was convinced. It is also possible that he is not working alone but as part of a conspiracy, and that too we must ascertain."

"Why, do you think, were the murders committed so quickly, so close together?"

"I can only imagine that the killer has some sort of time limit, a date by when all his victims must be dispatched. Alternatively, it is possible that the times were chosen because all three were available to him then, relatively easily. This may become clearer as our investigation proceeds."

"Or tomorrow, if Miss Scanlon has something new for us."

Holmes laughed harshly. "I shall be most surprised, if we see her there tomorrow. It is doubtful, I think, if she is aware of our appointment." He saw the confusion in my face, and immediately explained. "We must both ensure that we are armed when we attend Resurrection Church Hall, for it is surely a trap. How can it be otherwise, for what purpose would she have in meeting us there when a return to Harrow would be mutually more convenient?"

"Perhaps she has discovered that the presiding priest is somehow involved, or possesses useful information."

"That is highly unlikely, old fellow, since Resurrection Church Hall has been derelict for the last few years. As I recall, the roof was struck by lightning during a storm and never repaired, since most of the former congregation had transferred their attendance to a new and much grander structure a few miles away. If you recall, Mr Josiah Endicott's visit to Miss Scanlon resulted in an attack upon his person. Now that we have interviewed her we appear to be subject to similar, but I suspect more severe, retaliation by means of whatever awaits us at Resurrection Church Hall, from either Doctor Andovene, his accomplices or more hired roughs."

"But Holmes," I began, astounded that he intended to place us in such peril, "we could easily be killed. We should inform Scotland Yard, and let them make arrests."

"Our adversaries would see their approach from afar, and be gone before they entered the scene. Also, you will recall that our client has already consulted Gregson, without result or interest. This would hardly be the first time that we have faced an uncertain situation together, but if my strategy is not to your taste I will go alone."

"I will ensure that my service weapon is fully loaded, and that my pocket contains spare ammunition."

Holmes smiled. "I thought I knew my Watson."

The following morning our breakfasts were consumed quickly, to Mrs Hudson's dismay. We departed immediately and procured a hansom which left us at Hampstead Heath ten minutes before the appointed time.

"I believe this to be the place we seek, Watson, the stone structure at the junction of this lane and the other that intersects it."

I peered in the direction that he had indicated. "It does indeed appear disused. The small forest of surrounding oaks partially hides its condition."

"No doubt our adversaries will make use of that concealment, but we will wait for them to reveal themselves."

We walked along the short neglected path that took us from the lane to the tall doors. I drew my revolver and looked around us as Holmes struggled to force our entrance. The rusted hinges protested loudly but yielded to his strong grip, and we passed through the narrow gap thus created into the interior.

Sunlight streaked through the ruined roof, casting shapes and patterns upon the crumbling stone walls. Holmes produced his weapon as a sharp cry reached us, but it was nothing more than startled birds who had nested in the rafters above. That this had once been a place of worship was plain to see, but the dust of recent years had settled thickly upon the altar and the broken remains of rows of seats.

"Someone has used this place as a wine cellar," I observed. "There are rows of kegs stacked against the wall."

"They have not been here for long, since no dust has yet settled upon them. There appears to be no other entrance, and no windows apart from the high row of arrow-slits along the opposite wall. This is an old place indeed but there is a strong smell of lamp oil or something similar, which also suggests recent occupation."

The echo of his voice faded, and for several minutes nothing more intruded upon the silence.

"You were right about this place, Holmes, for there is certainly no sign of Miss Scanlon or anyone else."

At that moment we were startled by the loud report of the doors slamming shut behind us.

"Ah, our confrontation begins," he said calmly.

In an instant we had thrown ourselves to the floor, an instinctive response to the hail of bullets that ricocheted around us. We took cover behind the remains of a row of seats, before realising that the target was not us, but the stack of wooden kegs close by.

"There, Watson, the arrow-slits!"

I followed his gaze and saw the dim silhouettes of two marksmen framed against the narrow apertures. We returned fire immediately, and heard a sharp cry as one of our bullets found its mark and the shots ceased abruptly. I heard a new sound and turned to see that the kegs now leaked profusely, quickly saturating the remains of the carpet along the aisle.

"Holmes, I cannot breathe!"

"That substance exudes a heavy gas. Back to the door, quickly!"

"They may be waiting there for us. We could walk into a fusillade."

He took me by the arm, coughing. "We have no choice. Worse is coming."

We stumbled back the way we had come, and a moment later I saw what it was that my friend had anticipated. As we reached the entrance something was forced through an arrow-slit above, something aflame and burning rapidly. As it fell to the floor, it ignited the spreading chemical and became a wall of fire that engulfed the carpet and broken seats as we watched. I could taste the gas and began to breathe shallowly, as did Holmes, and racking coughs possessed us both.

I grasped the door-latch and attempted to force it, but it was immovable. Three bullets from my revolver caused the handle to turn freely, but the latch did not lift. Holmes had placed a handkerchief over his mouth and nose and now delivered a hard kick to the rotting planks, and I assisted him. I was near to being convinced that our last moments had come, when a long split appeared. Still starved of air, we rained blows upon it until I feared that our boots would take no more, but the gap grew wider until he seized a broken plank with both hands and tore it out, and then another. We pushed our heads through the widened hole to take in air, then ripped more wood away until we were able to climb through the resulting jagged space. We staggered a few yards, relieved that our adversaries were nowhere to be seen, and taking in gulps of revitalising air.

We both looked along the lane, as a coach faded quickly into the distance.

"Either they believe we are dead, or they have postponed the battle to another time," he remarked as we peered around the corner of the building with our weapons ready. Two tall ladders stood propped against the wall, and smoke poured from the arrow-slits in clouds.

"We can expect a long walk from here, Holmes. There is no sign of a hansom."

"I shall be surprised if we do not find one within ten minutes. If we continue along this road, we will arrive at its junction with the main road to Highgate, where transport is plentiful."

My friend was soon proven correct, and he surprised me by giving the cabby instructions to take us to Harrow, rather than Baker Street.

"But why are we visiting Miss Scanlon again?" I asked. "You stated with certainty that she had no hand in summoning us to Resurrection Church Hall."

Holmes steadied himself, as the hansom passed oven an uneven patch of road. "Quite so, but our adversaries have twice had to act as a result of information that she has disclosed. It may be that they believe she gleaned more knowledge from her friendship with Doctor Andovene than is actually true. That they have probably decided to permanently close this threat to their security seems to me to be likely."

"You believe that they could have murdered her?" Despite the late morning warmth, I felt suddenly cold.

"Or kidnapped her, yes. However, if they have not been so quick to act we may be in time."

Sadly, Holmes was again correct. We arrived at Miss Scanlon's cottage and he requested that our driver wait. His expression became grim when, instead of rapping on the door with his stick, he turned the handle and it swung open. With our weapons in hand we entered cautiously, soon to discover the poor girl's body lying at the foot of the stairs.

"Her neck is broken," I observed. "Clearly, she lost her footing as she descended. The carpet, as we see, is wrinkled halfway down the staircase. It appears that our adversaries had no hand in this."

Holmes was silent as he studied the scene. "Much to the contrary, Watson, it is evident that she was murdered. Our enemies wish us to believe that the fall was accidental, that is all."

"You have seen indications of this?"

"One can hardly miss them. Look carefully at Miss Scanlon's upper arms, which are bruised from her assailant's grip as he forced her to the top of the staircase. Note also that her bodice is ripped above the waist, by which she would have first been restrained as she suffered the onset of panic upon realising what was about to happen to her. Finally, the stair covering has been disturbed in a most unlikely place. I cannot imagine her placing a foot in that position during a normal descent." He shook his head sadly. "I feel I am responsible for this, Watson, to some extent."

I looked at him curiously, appalled by such a conclusion. "But how can that be?"

"From the swift action by our adversaries following Mr Josiah Endicott's visit, and the telegram to Baker Street a few hours after our presence here, it was obvious that Miss Scanlon was under their observation, probably from afar since I saw no indication of it. I feel I should have arranged some form of protection for her, that may have saved her life."

"Holmes, Scotland Yard has already refused to take action. What could you have done?"

"I could have despatched you to watch the watchers, or sent Barker. As a private agent, he is skilled in such things."

During the journey back to our lodgings, he said little else. He requested our driver to stop once, I suspect to despatch a telegram to Gregson advising him of the developments in the case, although he did not confide this to me.

Luncheon was a solemn affair, and it was clear that he still reproached himself. Our landlady looked with disapproval at his hardly-touched food.

When she had left us we repaired to our armchairs as was our custom. Holmes selected his cherrywood pipe and spent some little time exhaling clouds of fragrant smoke. I consumed a Turkish cigarette as he considered how we should proceed.

"According to our client's notes," he said at last, "the first murder, that of Mrs Helena Court, took place in a carriage of the *London Express* shortly before it arrived at Paddington. Mr Endicott records that the railway attendant, Mr Enoch Watts, was interviewed by Scotland Yard, although nothing useful resulted. I think we will visit Paddington Station this afternoon, Watson, to see if Mr Watts can be found."

Later, Holmes paid off the hansom and we made our way through the lingering crowd, some waiting to board a train while others were there to meet arriving passengers, to the station master's office. There, the rather jovial occupant consulted a time-table and a list, presumably of employees, in order to inform us that the train in the care of Mr Watts would be arriving in fifty-seven minutes. After thanking him we made use of a bench on the platform, and Holmes used the time to explain that, although he had not yet developed a definite theory, he was convinced that we were dealing with something far deeper here, with adversaries more formidable than he had at first thought.

I consulted my pocket-watch as a train sped into the station. We rose at once, and walked alongside the coaches, tasting smoke as passengers poured onto the platform. Holmes espied a young attendant, and enquired about Mr Watts.

"The other end of the train, sir. That's Enoch's patch."

We advanced until the tender, still high with coal, was all that separated the coach we boarded from the engine. It was now quite empty, save for an elderly man in railway uniform who was busy sweeping the aisle.

He looked up, surprised that there should be boarders when the train had reached its destination, and stopped to lean on his broom.

"Can I assist you gentlemen?"

"That is our hope," said Holmes, before introducing us. "We are continuing an investigation into the death of a woman last week, on board a train on which you worked at the time."

Mr Watts brushed a stray lock of white hair back from his brow. "Yes, indeed sir. It was I that found her as I came down to the rear coach. It was murder all right, a knife was stuck in the poor lady's chest and fresh blood had soaked the front of her costume."

"I understand that Scotland Yard was called in."

"As soon as I could, I reported to the station master who telegraphed the Yard immediately. I did my best to keep the other passengers away from her compartment, and drew the blinds straight away. What steps the police have since taken, I do not know."

Holmes nodded. "Did you not request the aid of someone else?"

"That would be the gentleman in the next compartment. He was there alone, just as the murdered lady had been in hers. He wasn't keen on giving me a hand at first, so that I had to practically plead with him."

At the far side of the tracks another train arrived, the scream of its brakes deafening. As coach doors were slammed back, a surge of those waiting to board was delayed by alighting passengers. Mr Watts glanced briefly through the window at the spectacle, but Holmes' gaze did not leave him.

"Pray tell us anything you can recall, about this man."

"Well, let me see," the railway official scratched his head. "His name was Mr Morton Coleridge, I know that because he gave me his card. He was a salesman for a company that makes false teeth you see sir, and I must have mentioned that mine have never fitted well. Apart from that he appeared quite overcome by the event, and was anxious to leave the train at the first possible moment because of an appointment."

"Did he do so before the arrival of assistance from Scotland Yard?"

"Oh yes, sir. There was no point in him staying, you see. He had heard nothing of the killing, and was as appalled as I was on hearing of it. He went off to his appointment, rather pale-faced."

"You have his whereabouts, you said?" I reminded him.

Mr Watts fumbled in a waistcoat pocket, then another, before handing Holmes a card that was slightly the worse for wear. My friend took it and glanced at the ornate script before returning it immediately.

"Our thanks to you, Mr Watts, your assistance has been invaluable."

"Very glad I was able to help, sir," he replied as my friend slipped him a half-sovereign, "very glad indeed."

"We have, I think, enough time to visit Mr Moreton Coleridge before we return to Baker Street for dinner," Holmes remarked as we left the station.

"You believe then, that he may have something significant to tell us?"

"It occurred to me as a possibility. You will recall that Mr Watts noticed that Mrs Court's blood from her wound was *fresh*, which means of course that the murder was committed shortly before its discovery. He mentioned that he approached the rear coach, yet said nothing of passing anyone who, in retrospect, could have aroused his suspicions. Possibly then, the murderer made off in the other direction, passed Mr Coleridge's compartment and attracted a fleeting glimpse while on his way to wherever he concealed himself until the train came to rest. In any event, I cannot believe that Mr Coleridge would hear nothing from such a short distance while a woman was being stabbed in such a brutal manner. A scream of terror or surprise should have alerted him."

"Unless the murderer was able to place a hand across her mouth, preventing such a response."

"That is, of course, possible, although I would have expected most women to cry out before this could be achieved, as soon the intention to assault became apparent. However, we may soon be able to draw our own conclusions."

"Mr Coleridge lives nearby, then?"

"In Glastonbury Crescent, which is off Tottenham Court Road. Cheer up, Watson, you will not miss your dinner, I promise you."

Chapter Three – A Strange Little Man, and Some Complications

We walked in companionable silence for a short while, with Holmes seemingly oblivious to everything save his own thoughts. The sounds from Paddington Station were hardly discernible, by the time we were able to secure a hansom.

The residence we sought was a narrow house in the middle of a half-moon shaped enclave. Mr Coleridge proved to be a small, balding man with a furtive and sly disposition. I sensed, as Holmes introduced us and explained the purpose of our visit, my friend's dislike or disapproval of the man. I confess, although it is not usually my way, to instant and similar feelings, as we were led into a grim and untidy parlour.

Our host made no offer of refreshments, and we seated ourselves in worn armchairs around a fireplace which appeared to contain the remains of kindling several days old.

"I do not employ servants," Mr Coleridge said as if he had read my thoughts. "My life is simple, and I avoid unnecessary expense." He crossed his legs and immediately uncrossed them nervously, shifting his position in his chair. "What is it about the events on that train that you gentlemen believe I can provide assistance with? Please be brief, as I have an appointment which I must not fail to keep."

"I understand that you are an agent for a concern manufacturing false teeth," said Holmes, beginning in a way that surprised me.

"That is so. It does not pay well, but I will not starve. But how is that connected with the murder of that woman?"

Holmes shrugged. "I only mention it because the railway attendant attached some importance to it."

"Ah yes. I recommended that he call at our premises, when he is able. I am certain that we can improve upon his current dental situation."

"As to the train," Holmes returned, "I would be obliged if you would cast your mind back. You have already stated that you heard nothing, although the murder took place in the next compartment to your own, but it occurred to me that you may have seen the killer as he left. I have already established that he could not have departed in the opposite direction, that is towards the front of the train, so he has to have passed your window. Is it possible that you heard someone in the corridor, when the shutter was not closed?"

Mr Coleridge was silent for a moment, and appeared more anxious and uncertain still. "I have a vague impression of a large man, dressed in a black frock coat and top hat, bustling along outside my compartment. I did indeed look up from my book and catch sight of him briefly through the window. He was gone in an instant."

"Do you recall anything of his appearance?"

"Only that he had a full black beard and rather cruel eyes. I had no reason to suspect that I would be called upon to remember him."

"You did not see where he was bound for?" I asked. "For example, a nearby compartment."

Mr Coleridge shook his head. "I believe there were no more compartments, further back in the train than my own. Perhaps he sought concealment and refuge in the guard's van, though I am unsure as to whether it is possible to gain direct access to there from a passenger coach." He produced his pocket-watch and favoured it with a quick glance. "But now, Gentlemen, I must request that you excuse me. The appointment I referred to earlier is now imminent, and I have still to complete my preparations."

Holmes, hat in hand, rose from his chair an instant before myself. "Thank you, Mr Coleridge, for a most enlightening interview. No, do not accompany us, sir, but continue to prepare for your guest. We will see ourselves out."

Near the junction of Glastonbury Crescent, almost at the point where it gave onto Tottenham Court Road, two large oaks had spread their branches wide. When a glance around us revealed that we were alone, we concealed ourselves behind the thick trunks so that we could not be seen from Mr Coleridge's house.

"What are you expecting to see, Holmes?" I enquired curiously.

"Nothing at all, if I am not mistaken."

"But Mr Coleridge is expecting a guest. He laid much emphasis on the importance of the appointment."

"Precisely. A few moments of patience will, I think, reveal the truth of my suspicions."

We remained there for an uneventful fifteen minutes, then Holmes indicated that we should continue as if there had been no interruption. No sooner than we had entered Tottenham Court Road than a cab appeared, and we were quickly on our way back to Baker Street.

"I imagine that we waited to discover the identity of Mr Coleridge's visitor?" I ventured as the horse broke into a trot.

"Not so. I wished to confirm that there was no appointment."

"Mr Coleridge seemed quite unnerved at the prospect of our interruption to his arrangements."

"It was an invention, to rid himself of us at the earliest opportunity, nothing more."

"He was obviously very uncomfortable, confronted with our questions."

We steadied ourselves, as the hansom was brought to a sudden halt. I looked out to see an urchin scurry across the road before us.

"Indeed he was, but not," Holmes said, "because of anything connected with the murder. As we entered that short corridor leading to the parlour I chanced to glance into another room as the door had been left ajar. There I saw several piles of money arranged on a table, obviously being prepared for deposit in a bank or similar institution. At first I thought Mr Coleridge to be a miser, but his determination to be rid of us at the earliest moment and his evident discomfort persuaded me that he is probably guilty of embezzlement. However, nothing can be done without proof, and we have more important matters to hand."

"I noticed how, despite his insistence that he saw nothing, he was able to give quite a detailed description of another passenger who could well be the murderer of Mrs Court."

Holmes nodded. "Mr Coleridge may have been engaged in something unlawful, possibly counting some of his ill-gotten gains from that day's work. Hence he would have maintained watchfulness of anyone nearby. Any stranger who came near could be, in those circumstances, a threat in the shape of a member of the plain-clothes official force, or a private agent."

At that we lapsed into silence until our arrival at our lodgings. Mrs Hudson's roast beef was beautifully cooked, but Holmes did not share my enthusiasm. He ate absently, his mind elsewhere, hardly sampling the steamed pudding afterwards but pouring strong coffee for us both as soon as it was brought.

"I think, Watson," he began when we were settled in our armchairs and had smoked a first pipe, "that we must face this problem from a different direction. We have founded our investigation thus far upon the deaths of Mr Seth Cornwell, and Mrs Helena Court. Tomorrow I propose to look into the murder of the third victim, Mr Jude Groat."

The following morning Holmes took to his armchair immediately after breakfast. Resuming his study of Mr Endicott's notes he appeared too absorbed to look up as Mrs Hudson entered our sitting-room to clear away the remains of our meal, and so it was I who held open the door for the laden lady's exit.

"My dear Holmes," I remarked. "Your mind is in another place."

He glanced at me as a thin smile crept into his expression. "How right you are, Watson. It is in the Experience Club, to be precise. Mr Endicott records the murder of Mr Jude Groat as taking place in the smoking room there. It seems that the killer was unknown, and promptly made a successful exit. He has so far remained at liberty."

"I was under the impression that membership was necessary, in order to attend these Pall Mall clubs. How was Mr Groat killed?"

"Shot through the heart with a small calibre weapon. He was sitting, apparently, no more than a few feet from his murderer, who then fled before any of those present could recover from the shock."

"So we are to visit the Experience Club, this morning?"

"That would be appropriate, I think. These notes state that Mr Groat had two close friends who reside there for most of the year, Mr Vern Fuller and Mr Andrew Tomkins. I understand that this was learned from the contents of the dead man's pocket book, rather than other club members who were in attendance at the time. As usual with other such institutions, the club protects the privacy of its own."

"This murderer had the devil's own luck, to escape in such a manner."

"Indeed." He strode to the hat-stand and retrieved our hats and coats. "But let us see what can be learned."

"At this time of the morning? Would an evening visit not be more likely to find these gentlemen at home?"

"If they reside at the club we will likely find them having just finished breakfast. Besides, I am curious to discover the nature of the establishment. It has a reputation as the haunt of eccentrics and would-be heroes, many of whom drink at the expense of their fellows on the strength of the tales they repeatedly tell."

"A strange but harmless place, perhaps?"

"On that score, we shall see."

The traffic was annoyingly thick as we passed through St James in the City of Westminster. Our cab entered Pall Mall at the St James Street end and proceeded towards Trafalgar Square. I noted the Reform Club, the Athenaeum and the Diogenes Club before, almost at the extent of the thoroughfare, our driver brought his aging horse to a gentle halt.

Holmes paid the cabby, who set off immediately towards a fellow loitering further along the street, clearly seeking transportation. We stood before a three-storey building, fronted by tall double-doors and identified by a shining brass plate.

My friend rang the door-bell, and we waited. Presently a thin elderly man in the uniform of a club steward emerged to peer down at us from the top of the short flight of steps.

He scrutinised first me, and then Holmes. "Yes, gentlemen?"

"We are pursuing a police investigation," Holmes replied. "It is of the utmost importance that we speak to Mr Vern Fuller and Mr Andrew Tomkins, without delay. Kindly deliver this to one or other of these gentlemen."

The steward accepted Holmes' card, his lack of expression reminding me of the mannequins on display at my tailor's. "I fear that *Colonel* Tomkins and Mr Fuller are still at breakfast, sir. Whether they will be available later, I cannot say. Perhaps you would care to leave a message?"

"I have already indicated that this is police business. Its nature is urgent."

"But your card says," he made a pretence of reading it again, "that you are a 'consulting detective', does it not? I understand that to mean that you have no official standing. If you were to return accompanied by an officer of Scotland Yard, that would be a different matter. As it is, gentlemen, I bid you good-day."

The door was closed swiftly and silently.

"A very rude fellow!" I exclaimed. "His condition to admit us will be difficult to meet, since the Yard, according to our client, currently treats this as a case of little importance."

Holmes was unperturbed. "We have met similar situations before now. Brother Mycroft can usually provide some sort of key."

"The Diogenes Club is but a stone's throw away."

"True, but my brother is most likely at his desk in Whitehall, as the hour for luncheon approaches. However, if we interrupt our journey back to Baker Street to dispatch a telegram, we may hear from him later. But here comes a cab, Watson, be good enough to raise your walking-cane. Ah yes, the driver is already reining in his horse."

We paused once, as Holmes had intended, at a small Post Office near the National Gallery. My friend seemed excessively jovial during luncheon, and consumed his roast pheasant with relish. I concluded that he was confident that we would gain entrance, through Mycroft, to the Experience Club, and that he awaited the interviews with the friends of Mr Jude Groat eagerly.

We had hardly left the dining-table when the door-bell rang. It crossed my mind that we might be about to be presented with a new case but then, as I am sure that Holmes had already discerned, the footsteps of our landlady, unaccompanied upon the stairs, suggested that it was a message that she brought.

Mrs Hudson offered Holmes a yellow envelope on a tray, and then withdrew. He slit it open with a thumbnail and glanced at the telegram within.

"Ha! We are fortunate, Watson, in that Mycroft has invited me to his office this afternoon." He rose and snatched up his hat and coat. "If I am quick, and a cab is forthcoming, I can be in Whitehall at the time he stipulates. I do not anticipate a long absence, old fellow, but should it turn out that way, pray ask Mrs Hudson to keep my dinner warm."

With that he was gone. From the window I saw him board a hansom almost immediately, before I settled in my chair with the mid-day edition of *The Daily News*.

I was surprised when he returned in less than two hours.

"I had expected you to be away longer, since you have not seen your brother for some little time."

Holmes wore a mildly concerned expression. "There is something peculiar here, Watson. Something about which Mycroft is saying little. At my arrival I was shown into a tiny room containing nothing but a desk, two chairs and a portrait of our Queen. My brother listened to my request before demanding to know my reason for it, and lectured me to refrain from interfering. He consented to ease our entry into the Experience Club only after I persisted in my efforts. He said, resignedly, that he supposed I would find a way in with or without his help, even if it involved applying for membership."

"I cannot see how your brother is connected with this affair."

"Nor can I, as yet. I suspect that his reluctant agreement indicates that, far from aiding our investigation, Mycroft will ensure that we discover nothing that he wishes to keep hidden."

"So, we must wait for his instructions?"

"Not at all. After some deliberation, he suggested that you and I should present ourselves at the Experience Club again, this time to ask that rather uncouth steward to summon a Commander Bradbury who will sign us in as temporary members."

"When is this to be?"

"At eight o'clock sharp, this evening."

I nodded. "Then I have time to finish this article, before dinner."

"And I to conduct a search of my index."

In such ways we filled the remaining time before changing for dinner. Mrs Hudson served a veal and ham pie which I did justice to, while Holmes ate sparingly. I knew that his mind was on what lay before us and his brother's concerns, and it did not surprise me when he jumped to his feet the moment our meal was concluded.

"Come, Watson, we cannot afford to be late. Mycroft was most emphatic on that point."

We were fortunate in that a hansom presented itself quickly. Holmes instructed the driver to deliver us a short distance from our actual destination, so that a brisk walk would bring us to the Experience Club almost exactly at the appointed time.

On this occasion it was unnecessary to ring the door-bell, as a different steward was in the act of showing out a gentlemen as we approached.

"I understand that Commander Bradbury is expecting us," Holmes told the steward as the departing member searched for a hansom.

"Indeed, sir. You gentlemen then, are Mr Sherlock Holmes and Doctor Watson?"

"We are."

The man bowed respectfully. "If you would care to wait in the foyer, I will send the Commander to you."

We thanked him and he entered one of the long corridors that led off a small circular foyer. Several minutes passed, before a tall, bald man with a magnificent moustache smilingly approached us.

"Gentlemen, I am a member," he said after introductions had been made, "but tonight I am here specifically at the bidding of Mr Mycroft Holmes. I have already ensured that your entry is approved. As I understand it, you wish to speak to Mr Vern Fuller and Colonel Andrew Tomkins, both of whom I have observed in the smoking room." Like ourselves, the Commander wore evening dress, and his row of medals glinted in the harsh gas-light. "If you enter the corridor over there, near the marble bust of Caesar, you will find that the third door on your left will admit you to the smoking room, the place you seek." He cast a glance in that direction. "Before I leave, is there anything more that you require?"

Holmes took in our surroundings, noting the constant comings-and-goings between the doors and corridors. "I think not, Commander, save to express our thanks and to request that you convey them to my brother. Good evening to you."

He replied and left us, making off in the direction of the exit. Somewhat relieved, I thought.

"A pleasant sort, Holmes."

"Pah! He is one of Mycroft's more amiable lackeys," he replied sourly. "Let us follow his directions to the smoking room which, if you recall, is also the room where Mr Jude Groat was shot. I am curious to see more of this place."

We strode across the foyer, our footsteps echoing beneath the voluminous domed roof, and approached the door that had been indicated to us. Holmes opened it and I caught a glimpse of a wide, smoke-filled chamber with scattered tables occupied by men absorbed in conversation or sitting alone. I took in the long bar, tended by two men working constantly, before he said in a low voice:

"Ah, already I see things much more clearly, Watson."

Completely puzzled, I followed him in.

"My dear Holmes," I retorted. "What can you mean. I saw nothing of significance."

"That is because you did not know what to look for. Those gentlemen over there, unless I am much mistaken, are the ones whom we seek."

We approached their table, and I studied the two men as we did so. Mr Vern Fuller was short and squat with side-whiskers that extended to his jaw-bones and unruly black hair, while his tall companion sat ramrod-straight in a way that betrayed his connection to the military.

"Good evening, gentlemen," began Holmes. "My name is Sherlock Holmes and this is my friend and colleague, Doctor John Watson. We are continuing a police enquiry into three murders which took place several days ago. As you are friends of one of the victims, Mr Jude Groat, we believe you may be able to assist us."

Both men regarded us silently for a moment, then Mr Fuller responded. "We had been informed that two strangers desired to speak to us here, though not of the reason. You must wield considerable influence in some quarters, to be admitted without membership."

"We had assumed that the men seeking us were fellow members," added Colonel Tomkins.

Holmes shrugged. "I imagine Scotland Yard were involved in the arrangement. The details were not shared with us."

The two men glanced at each other briefly, and I seized the instant of silence between us to settle the question in my mind.

"As you have discerned, we are unfamiliar with the club. I am curious to know why it is so-called."

"The answer to that is absurdly simple," Mr Fuller replied. "In order to qualify for membership, an applicant has to have had at least one experience of note, preferably in a foreign land. In my own case, I was fortunate enough to be on hand to save the life of the Duke of Mellerton, as a member of his exploratory expedition in the jungles of Peru. Our quest was to discover a legendary lost tribe, but the poor fellow almost drowned in a treacherous whirlpool."

"And I was part of the supporting force in the colonisation of Eastern Africa," Colonel Tomkins volunteered. "Later to be instrumental in the establishment of the trade route through the port of Mombasa. My comrades and I faced many difficulties, but we prevailed eventually."

"Have you ever visited South Africa?" Holmes asked unexpectedly.

"I had intended to travel a great deal more across the continent, but I was recalled."

"And your friend, Mr Jude Groat, how did he come to join the club?"

"Mr Groat was a very private man, but he did relate to me on one occasion how he fought off a tiger with nothing more than a staff, during the Maharajah of Nimpoor's hunt of a few years ago."

Holmes nodded. "Our information is that you two gentlemen were his closest friends, within the club."

"I suppose that is true," Mr Fuller answered. "At any rate, I have rarely seen him converse with any of the other members, save to exchange a remark or two. He kept his own counsel for much of the time, making it impossible to get to know him well, although at various times he mentioned that he was unmarried and had no financial difficulties. I believe him to have been a member here since the autumn of two years ago, just a little less than Colonel Tomkins and myself."

"Were either of you gentlemen present when Mr Groat was murdered?"

"That occurred, as you may know, in this very room." Colonel Tomkins reminded us. "We were in the restaurant at the time and we heard the shot, although we did not at first recognise it as such. I understand that the fellow responsible rushed out into the street before anyone could prevent him, while poor Groat lay dying. How he gained entry in the first place has yet to be discovered." "We can but hope that this will come to light in due course. Are you acquainted, or do you know if Mr Groat was, with either Mrs Helena Court or Mr Seth Cornwell?"

The two men shook their heads.

"Those names appeared in the newspapers," remembered Mr Fuller. "They were killed at almost the same time as our friend. But there can be no connection, surely?"

"Apparently not."

During our conversation the noise in the room seemed to have abated, but now it rose again with the entrance of a member who seemed popular with everyone. The drifting cigar and pipe smoke thickened above us, and fits of coughing broke out briefly in one place after another. One of the men in charge of the bar emerged to collect empty glasses, and I noticed for the first time that a full and uncorked bottle of Alsace red had remained without attention between the colonel and Mr Fuller throughout our conversation. I wondered if Holmes would interpret this as a sign that the men had been tense and on their guard.

He glanced past them to a nearby display of photographic portraits, arranged on a wall. "That picture at the end of the first row. The likenesses are of you gentlemen, are they not?"

Mr Fuller turned to look. "Certainly."

"And is the third man Mr Jude Groat?"

"It is. The occasion was shortly after our first meeting, soon after he became a member here."

Holmes got to his feet suddenly. "My thanks to you, gentlemen. I found our conversation most informative."

We took our leave and made our way out of the club. On the way, my friend paused momentarily to scrutinise the picture at close quarters. He said not a word until we were aboard a hansom and on our way back to our lodgings.

"A most satisfactory evening," he said, emerging from a reverie. "We can safely say that we now know much more about this affair, Watson."

I looked across at him, bewildered. "I confess to having learned nothing, except a few unimportant facts."

"A rare thing indeed, is a totally unimportant fact, as I have mentioned before now. Extend your patience a little further, until we are taking a glass of brandy in our sitting-room, and I will make known to you all that I have observed."

We arrived shortly afterwards. As we sipped the harsh spirit, I reflected upon our visit.

"You seemed suddenly enlightened, the moment we entered the smoking room," I remembered.

"No doubt you found that confusing," Holmes moved his thin form to a more comfortable position, now sitting upright in his chair. "Do you recall the young gentleman at the table directly behind that of Mr Fuller and Colonel Tomkins?"

"Vaguely. He was sitting alone, I think."

"Quite so. He was disguised, but I once saw a picture of him at Scotland Yard. His torn ear lobe identified him instantly."

"But who was he?"

"His name is Otto Klein, regardless of what he calls himself now, one of the most dangerous of the group of Imperial German spies currently in England. At the sight of him I became certain who our adversaries are and, although I cannot yet prove it, of the true identity of 'Doctor Andovene', as well as that of the murderer of Mrs Helena Court and Mr Jude Groat. Klein's ruthless reputation is suggestive of it. Further, I observed how the upper portion of Klein's face was slightly tanned. The paler jawbone area suggests that a beard was shaved off recently. You will recall that Mr Coleridge described the man he saw after Mrs Court's murder as being heavily bearded."

"Great Scott, Holmes! Could we not have summoned the Yard, or your brother's people?"

He shook his head. "I see now that it was precisely because he feared such an act that Mycroft resented our intervention and was so reluctant to assist. He doubtlessly sees this as part of a much larger plot that he will foil when the time is right."

"Was that how you were able to identify Mr Fuller and Colonel Tomkins, because you realised that this man Klein was positioned to watch and overhear their conversation?"

"Unless Klein was doing this without their knowledge, it was obvious that they must be part of the spy ring also. To test this I listened for faint traces of Germanic accents in the speech of both men. With Mr Fuller it was imperceptible, but with Colonel Tomkins relatively noticeable at times. You will recall that I enquired whether he had visited South Africa."

"I wondered why, at the time."

"It was because there is a significant German presence there, they are interested in minerals and gold, and it seemed likely to have been the true reason for him to have been sent to that continent. Doubtlessly he was there to observe British activities, also."

"So the tales of Mombasa, and Peru, were false?"

"I would imagine that some of their qualifications for membership of the Experience Club are false, at least. I suspect that they had previously ascertained that the club does not enquire too deeply into its members' veracity, or had made extensive arrangements to satisfy such conditions."

"It struck me as impolite that we were not invited to sit, much less offered a glass of wine."

"It is not unknown for the higher ranks of the German military, as well as other services, to treat those that they regard as enemies of the Kaiser's ideals as inferior."

"Uncouth, indeed," I scowled.

"The picture also was significant," he continued. "You will doubtless remember that it was stated to have been taken two years ago in the autumn, and shortly after Mr Groat became a member. It was also mentioned that those other two beauties had been members for not much longer."

"So it was said."

"The picture tells us at once that this is quite impossible. The flowers in the background were of the *fabaceae* genus, commonly called 'Wisteria'. At the end of summer, they would no longer be blossoming, but be well into their decline."

As on many occasions past, I marvelled at my friend's abilities, unique in my experience, to glean so much from what to me was so little. Inwardly, I rebuked myself for being oblivious to so much that was glaringly apparent once he had explained his interpretation.

He rose abruptly. "But now, old fellow, I will wish you good-night. By the time our breakfast is over in the morning, I will have decided upon a course to further our investigation."

Before I could replace my empty glass he was gone. After a moment I yawned and stretched and retired to my room also.

As it happened, I had scarcely finished my bacon and eggs before Holmes appeared. That he had risen before me I already knew, since the remains of his breakfast had littered the table until Mrs Hudson removed them as she brought my coffee.

As he ascended the stairs, I wondered what he had learned.

"I was surprised to see that you had already gone out, Holmes," I said as he hung up his hat and coat. "An urgent matter, I presume?"

"It concerned our protection."

"From what, or whom?"

He sat down opposite me, pouring both of us a fresh cup of coffee. "You cannot, surely, have taken our adversaries of last night to be fools. They now know that our attentions are directed at them, and that we will not desist until this affair is concluded to our satisfaction. Therefore they will act to prevent further interference to their purpose, whatever that may be. Let us not forget that these are professional agents of Imperial Germany, and enemies of our country. To involve three, perhaps more, of the spy ring, their objective must be of considerable magnitude and importance, and they will not take likely the threat that they perceive us to be."

His meaning was all too clear to me. "Do you suspect that our lives are in danger?"

"Of course. I went out in order to confirm that our lodgings are under observation and that we are to be followed when we venture out. Do not look so surprised, Watson, we have endured this situation before. The only uncertainty is whether they will arrange our demise to appear accidental, or if they intend an obvious crime. They may be willing to risk the attentions of Scotland Yard. It depends on how desperate they are to be free to continue their activities."

"Holmes, when did you realise that these murders were an international affair," I enquired as he filled his pipe with dark shag from the Persian slipper.

"I knew from the moment I saw Otto Klein, and then the picture at the Experience Club. You see, Watson, it came to me immediately that I had seen Mr Jude Groat before, although the name he used then was different. It was about two years ago, on the occasion of a visit to Mycroft's office in connection with a trifling affair which I had looked into on his behalf. Mr Groat was leaving as I arrived, and my brother stood in the doorway with him. Convention and good manners dictated that introductions be made although, as I have said, the name I was given was quite different."

"Good heavens, Holmes! Does this mean that Mr Groat was one of Mycroft's agents?"

"I cannot suppose otherwise, and my brother certainly has more close at hand. If we can make a connection between Mr Groat and the other victims, we may have a clearer insight as to the situation we now find ourselves involved in. Regarding Klein and his associates, I think we should be warned now. Ensure that you are armed at all times, as will I."

"How then, shall we proceed?"

He considered, briefly. "I have a mind to search the residence of Mrs Helena Court who, according to Mr Endicott's notes, was a widow who lived alone in the Southern

Hotel in Russell Square. On the way, we can dispense with or investigate any followers who may present themselves."

After a while, and nowhere near our destination, Holmes directed the cabby to stop. I looked in every direction as he paid the fare but could see nothing that presented a threat.

"We were not followed, after all," I said as the hansom disappeared into a side-street.

Holmes smiled faintly. "Much to the contrary, not only were we followed by a carriage separated from our hansom by three others, but someone leapt from it and concealed himself in a doorway as we alighted. Come, Watson, we will see if my knowledge of these tawdry backstreets will serve to rid us of our pursuers."

With me in his wake, he launched himself into an exploration of a maze of side-streets and narrow alleys. These were ill-kept and depressing places, where doors were painted in garish colours in an attempt to relieve the drabness and the atmosphere of sheer despair. We found ourselves in a high-walled street that appeared to have no exit, until Holmes turned suddenly into a narrow passage that had been invisible until we drew close.

"Quickly, step over this fence. He is not far behind us."

"But I saw no one."

"Nevertheless, he is there."

I obeyed, crossing the low barrier after him. We were now in a small enclosure with billowing sheets hanging from a clothes line stretching back to a crumbling terraced house. I saw that these probably shielded us from the observation of anyone within, as we left through a gate leading to a short path and thence to another street.

"Strathclyde Terrace," Holmes identified, "and still he persists. I fear that we have encountered someone with a knowledge of London equal to my own. You will recall that I mentioned that we should expect to be dealing with professionals."

"Wait, Holmes. Look!"

We had emerged into a long and curving thoroughfare. It appeared deserted and as dilapidated as the rest of the area which made the figure, top-hatted and in dark apparel, seem all the more out of place. He stood at the far end of the street, near where the houses began, unmoving and silent. After a moment he gave a low whistle, and pointed in our direction with his walking-cane. I felt Holmes stiffen beside me.

"This way, Watson. We may be able to outrun them."

We set off smartly in the other direction, but I soon realised that my friend had been wrong if he assumed that our pursuers would continue on foot. A four-in-hand coach now bore down on us at a speed that would surely overtake us before we could reach the junction ahead. We began to run. The thud of the hooves was like thunder in my ears, and the rate of approach increased rapidly. I heard clearly the crack of the whip and the snorting of the four black beasts as I realised that the narrow way before us would allow us no sanctuary. It came into my mind that if I were about to die, I could be in no better company than that of my friend.

Chapter 5 – Grim Tidings and Discoveries

Holmes had saved my life before now, but on this occasion it could truly be said that he snatched me from the jaws of death. The horses were all but upon us, the urgent cries of the coachman plain to hear, when we came to a dwelling that was clearly abandoned. Glass from the windows lay scattered across the pavement, and the remains of lace curtains hung in shreds. Seizing me by the arm, Holmes threw himself at the battered door. It collapsed under our combined weight and we fell on top of it as the coach sped past no more than a few feet away. As we lay in a dusty room I feared that the passengers would alight to find us helpless, presenting an easy kill for them. I felt for my service weapon, but there was no need - the horses had charged on without pause.

"Holmes! Are you injured?" I gasped.

He struggled to his feet, pulling me after him. "Bruises, I think, nothing more. I believe you have cut your hand."

"From a nail, protruding from the wreckage of that door. We must hurry, before they return."

With our revolvers at the ready we peered into the street. There was no sign of the coach, nor of the man who had followed us with such persistence. I caught sight of several faces watching us through grime-encrusted windows, but otherwise there was no sign of life.

"I cannot understand, as they were so intent on killing us, why they abandoned the chase," I said.

"Perhaps they intend to conduct a different offensive, later. Be assured that they will not desist."

I looked again, in both directions. "I think we should leave here quickly, Holmes."

"And so we shall. The appearance of this area suggests that it is unlikely that Russell Square is close at hand, but in fact it is less than half a mile away. Return your weapon to your pocket, but remain alert."

He then led us to the end of the street, afterwards taking a succession of crossings and turns that eventually saw us cautiously approaching a district of fine houses and open spaces where flowers bloomed abundantly. Holmes' eyes were everywhere, and it was not until he was satisfied that we were no longer pursued that we entered Russell Square.

"The building with the wide veranda and pillared entrance is the Southern Hotel, unless I am much mistaken," he observed. "Dust yourself down, Watson. Your coat looks almost as soiled as my own. It will not do for the *concierge* to mistake us for a couple of street beggars."

We restored our appearance as best we could, before climbing the short flight of steps and entering the cool interior of the hotel. Leading off the corridor was a spacious reading room, with aspidistras and other potted plants standing tall between the scattered armchairs. Uniformed staff circulated, bringing drinks to guests who reclined while burying themselves in the pages of *The Times* or *The Standard*.

"We are engaged in a continuation of a Scotland Yard enquiry," Holmes told the fellow behind the reception desk as he held out his card for examination. "Kindly confirm that the room formerly occupied by Mrs Helena Court has not been retaken."

The clerk consulted a thick ledger. "It is still as it was when it was examined by the police, sir. We received no instructions as to its further treatment as yet. It has not even been cleaned."

"Excellent. Pray let us have the key. I do not expect our business here to take long."

The clerk complied and directed us to the ornate staircase in the far corner. We reached the first floor and walked along a deserted passageway. Movement could be heard from behind some of the closed doors, and sounds from the restaurant below reached us faintly.

"Mrs Court was evidently sound financially," I remarked, "to have lived permanently in a hotel such as this. None of the guests down there appeared desperately in need of funds."

"I suspect that she had assistance to maintain her accommodation, but that has yet to be proved. Ah, this is her room."

He turned the key in the lock and we walked into a room that had its curtains closed. At a sign from Holmes I drew them to let light flood in on a scene which brought from him a scowl of disapproval.

"As I should have anticipated, Scotland Yard has trampled through here like a herd of horses."

He proceeded to kneel, and then to lie down upon the carpet, peering beneath the bed and all around the room from that level. From time to time, his murmurings told me that he had discovered something, but he did not speak until he had risen to his feet and again brushed dust from his morning-coat.

"Have you found anything of significance, Holmes?" I asked.

"A scrap of good quality notepaper."

"Nothing more?"

He smiled. "It is enough, perhaps, to be of some assistance."

I remained near the door, as he proceeded to examine the interior of the empty wardrobe and every drawer in the tall chest. He appeared to find nothing more, but sank into a brief but deeply thoughtful state.

"No, Watson, I fear we are too late," he said at last. "The lady's personal property was removed by Scotland Yard or someone else." He turned his head to again scrutinize every corner searching, I thought, for some avenue as yet unexplored. "There is no reason to suspect that Mrs Court was planning to leave here to live elsewhere, so it is all the more certain that she would have hidden..." He lapsed into another short silence. "Aha! There is but one possible hiding-place remaining."

With that he began, to my astonishment, an inspection of the bed-frame. Taking a coin from his pocket, he tapped the hollow metal at intervals while listening carefully. Finally, he put away the coin and grasped one of the brass knobs at the head of the bed. He attempted to turn it with some force, at first without result. Then it squeaked loudly and unscrewed, the knob coming free in his hand. He peered into the interior of the frame at the point of detachment, shaking his head. After restoring things to their previous state, he turned his attention to the knob at the other side of the bed. His expression lightened as he triumphantly withdrew a thin cylinder of paper.

"What have you discovered, Holmes?"

"Exactly what I expected to discover," he said as he ran his eyes over the unfolded sheet. He looked around the room once more. "But now there appears to be nothing more to be learned here. Time, I think, to return to Baker Street for luncheon, after which I will attempt to satisfy your curiosity. Things seem to be a little different from the impression I had first formed."

Mrs Hudson wore a faint air of disapproval as she served our meal. I concluded that it was because we had arrived back at our lodgings later than is usual, causing her the difficulty of keeping our food hot. I ate my devilled kidneys and roast potatoes with my usual relish, while Holmes consumed his portion more slowly while wearing an expression of deep contemplation.

When we were settled in our armchairs with the plates cleared away, he retrieved the scrap of paper he had discovered in Mrs Court's hotel room from his waistcoat pocket.

"I can see that this intrigues you, Watson. It confirmed a suspicion that was forming in my mind."

"You recognised the handwriting?"

"I did, at once."

"Was it that of someone from the Experience club?" Although I could not imagine how my friend could have seen a sample for comparison.

"Not at all. It was written by Mycroft."

"Your brother? We know of his connection with Mr Jude Groat, but how does that extend to Mrs Court?"

"After reading the paper that was hidden in the bed-frame, the conclusion is inescapable. A reconstruction of the situation is not difficult. It seems that she worked on the domestic staff at Buckingham Palace, regularly disclosing information regarding forthcoming events and the movements of the Royal family to Otto Klein, and possibly other members of the spy ring at the Experience Club."

"Good heavens! I had pitied that woman, and now we discover that she is a traitor."

"Not so. She first supplied the information to Mr Jude Groat, who we already know was one of Mycroft's agents, and he revised it, no doubt according to my brother's instructions, before it was passed to our German friends."

"A connection then, is established between Mr Groat and Mrs Court."

"So it is indicated from my reconstruction of things. It will now come as no surprise to discover that there is a link to Mr Seth Cornwell also, as our client surmised."

I believe that my friend would have said more, but at that moment the door-bell rang, interrupting him. We heard someone follow Mrs Hudson as she ascended the stairs, immediately before she showed Inspector Gregson into the room.

"Good afternoon, gentlemen," The Inspector said as our landlady withdrew.

"Gregson!" Holmes exclaimed. "What brings you here?"

Before replying our visitor sat at Holmes' bidding, and refused his offer of tea.

"To answer your question, sir, I have to enquire as to whether you are acquainted with Mr Moreton Coleridge."

"Indeed so. We visited him, in connection with a current investigation."

Gregson brushed away a stray lock of flaxen hair. "Would that be the affair also involving Mr Josiah Endicott?"

"It would. I understand that our client previously reported to you regarding several recent murders. He is now unable to pursue his own investigations as a private enquiry agent, because of injuries resulting from a violent attack upon his person."

"I learned little from his account, nor was I satisfied with his theory that the murders are in some way connected. My own enquiries are continuing. Tell me, Mr Holmes, when was it that you last saw Mr Coleridge?"

"The interview was two days ago."

"Did it result in anything to aid your investigation?"

Holmes shook his head. "He mentioned a fleeting encounter with a man who could have been Mrs Court's killer, aboard the train. Has he perhaps, remembered something more?"

"He has not," Gregson said grimly, "nor will he ever. He was found dead at his home this morning, by a postman seeking to deliver a package. It appears to be a case of suicide, but we will see what a post-mortem reveals."

I was shocked at this news, but Holmes appeared unaffected. "How did he die, inspector?"

"He took poison, apparently."

My mind immediately returned to Miss Daisy Scanlon's statement, and I knew that my friend would be thinking similarly.

"Was there any indication as to why he did this?"

"He left a note. It revealed two things: that he feared for his life from Mrs Court's murderer, who he had conversed with after the killing, and the identity of that murderer."

Holmes sat up straight in his chair. "Are you about to share that with us?"

"Certainly, Mr Holmes." The official detective allowed himself a faint and ironic smile. "He accuses Mr Josiah Endicott."

"So Mr Coleridge, fearing that the murderer of Mrs Court might suspect that he could be identified, would claim him as the next victim, decided to save him the trouble by taking his own life? Come now, inspector, you cannot believe that. The murderer clearly wishes to disguise his crime."

"Nevertheless, I felt bound to place Mr Endicott in custody. He informed me that you are working on his behalf."

"He was arrested with no evidence, other than the word of a man who cannot be questioned because he died by his own hand?"

"Not quite, Mr Holmes. I sent officers to search his rooms, and they returned with a locket which is believed to have belonged to Mrs Court, and a sample of the poison. Mr Endicott denies any knowledge of these, naturally. He cites an apparently purposeless recent break-in as the likely explanation of their presence."

"Doubtlessly this occurred since his visit to us. Perhaps it would be useful to compare that sample with the potion which caused the death of Mr Seth Cornwell."

"There is surely no connection."

"Perhaps not, but I should tell you that I have established such a link between Mr Jude Groat and Mrs Helena Court. These murders occurred in quick succession, did they not? If two are connected, then does it not seemed likely that the third is also?"

Gregson stood up. "I suppose it is possible, but I will continue to follow my own lines of enquiry. Now that I have informed you of the changed situation I will leave you gentlemen, and wish you good-day."

"My thanks to you, Inspector." Holmes said as we got to our feet. "I wish you well with your investigation. Between us we will yet throw light on this matter, never fear."

Gregson replied with a brisk nod, and left us.

"Do you think Otto Klein killed Mr Coleridge?" I asked when we were again seated.

Holmes considered for a moment. "Most likely. I shall be surprised if it turns out to be otherwise. The poison, I am certain, will be the same substance that was unwittingly administered to Mr Cornwell by Miss Scanlon. Our friends at the Experience Club are busily eliminating anyone who might conceivably furnish information about their activities to the official force, and possibly to us. Do not relax your guard for an instant, old fellow, our turn is coming soon."

"What of our client?"

"Mr Endicott will be questioned, and then released. He was not on that train, so he has nothing to fear. It should not take Scotland Yard long to ascertain this, so I am wondering why Klein and his friends have resorted to a strategy to disguise their guilt that can be so easily disproved. That, and the fact that the murders were committed is such rapid succession, again point to an underlying purpose of some urgency. Their ultimate goal behind all this will become apparent soon, I think."

"As I mentioned before, I have read of rumours of assassination plots concerning the Royal family and members of the government. If you recall, Mrs Court was passing information about Buckingham Palace to the spy ring via your brother's department."

"Excellent, Watson. That obvious connection had not escaped me. If these lives are in jeopardy, there is all the more reason to get to the bottom of this affair with all speed."

"For now, are we to attempt to discover the part that Mr Seth Cornwell has played in this?"

Holmes was silent for a moment. "We are, but on reflection I think it would be as well to first visit Mr Endicott after all. The workings of Scotland Yard are notoriously slow, and we may be able to hasten his release. If you will retrieve our hats and coats, a telegram to Gregson will be in order since he will have had our client kept in the cells until it can be decided whether the evidence against him is sufficient to proceed."

Our pleasant late afternoon walk took a little over half an hour. Holmes sent the telegram from the nearest Post Office, requesting leave to visit Mr Endicott at ten o'clock the following morning. He asked also that Inspector Gregson acknowledge this.

We arrived back at our lodgings to find that a package had arrived for Holmes during our absence. Our good landlady had kindly placed it in our room and appeared to tell us so as we ascended the stairs. Holmes thanked her and requested dinner in one hour. We closed the door behind us, shed our outer clothing and stood around the table he often used for his chemical experiments, staring at a box roughly a foot square encased in brown paper and tied with string.

"From a new client, perhaps?" I ventured.

"If that is so there will be an explanatory note inside, since we have received no telegram or letter to tell us to expect whatever this box contains. Be a good fellow, Watson, and go to your usual chair to light your last pipe before dinner. I will join you soon."

"You do not want me to see the contents?"

He smiled faintly. "I do not want you to be harmed, should this package be from our friends at the Experience Club. If they believe we are in any way a threat to their existence or their plans, they will certainly act against us as I have said."

Reluctantly, I obeyed. As I was about to be seated, he called across the room: "On second thoughts, stand near the window. The further away you are, the better, in case they have sent explosives."

Feeling a dreadful anticipation, I complied. He appeared absolutely calm as he carefully undid the string and discarded it, then unwrapped the paper slowly. A new, but very ordinary cardboard box stood before him. He took a backward pace and proceeded to walk around the table, viewing it from every angle. I struck a match and very nearly let it burn down to my fingers, such was my preoccupation with Holmes' actions. When the tobacco glowed and I had my first taste of the coarse shag, I watched him lift the lid cautiously. For some moments he stood perfectly still, before inserting both of his hands and slowly bringing out an object made of pewter or lead.

"A Buddha's head!" I cried. "Why on Earth would anyone send you such a thing? Is there no explanation enclosed?"

He turned it so that he could peer into its hollow innards. "No explanation is necessary," he said seriously. "Do not move from there until I have rendered it harmless."

"Be careful, Holmes!" It crossed my mind that a deadly creature, such as a spider or snake could be concealed within.

"There is nothing I can do," he decided after all as he replaced it in its box. "I will leave the box in the corner, for possible later examination. We must tell Mrs Hudson to on no account touch it."

"What does it contain, then?"

"Nothing. The Buddha head is completely hollow. If I placed my hand inside however, I feel certain that I would be a dead man shortly after."

"How so, if the thing is empty?"

He lowered the box, with its contents, to the floor. "You will have seen that I grasped it in both hands, to extract it from the box. The entire head is smothered with some sort of greasy substance that would prevent its handling with one hand only. How natural then, to insert a hand into the hollow interior which would allow a secure grip to be maintained."

I nodded. "What is the danger, then?"

"There is none, until the interior widens into the brain cavity. There, I saw that a sharpened ridge runs all around the edge. It would certainly have drawn blood, and I would be surprised if it were not impregnated with some deadly preparation that would do its work before help could be summoned."

"That is fiendish!" I retorted.

"And most indicative of our adversary's inventiveness and ruthlessness, wouldn't you say?" He smiled unexpectedly. "But cheer up, Watson. Their plan failed, this time, and I hear that our good landlady is already bringing our dinner."

Chapter Six – A Further Connection

The kedgeree was satisfying and every bit as good as those I remembered from my service in Afghanistan.

When the meal was concluded, Holmes and I settled ourselves before the fire as was our usual custom. As the evening progressed it had suddenly turned much colder, and our good landlady had lit the fire which now crackled and smoked as the dry kindling was consumed.

"So," I began as he lit his pipe from a glowing ember that he held in the fireside tongs, "I presume we are to visit the Yard in the morning, to attempt to assist our client."

"If Gregson will allow it."

"Let us hope that Mr Endicott can prove that he was elsewhere, at the time of Mrs Court's murder."

Holmes nodded. "I do not anticipate any great difficulty, there. Gregson, I suspect, made the arrest to demonstrate that he has made some progress in the case to his superiors, to pacify them while he searched for more substantial evidence. Hopefully, we will be able to place him on a more appropriate track soon."

"You do not appear much troubled, that our adversaries attempted to kill you, earlier."

"There would be little point in concerning ourselves unduly, I think. There is no way of defining when or how they will repeat their intentions, so we must be constantly on our guard."

"When we have established Mr Endicott's innocence, if that is possible, are we to return our attention to Mr Seth Cornwell?"

He rubbed his nose thoughtfully. "It would be as well, I think, to prove once and for all that the three murders are connected and originate from the same source."

"The Experience Club, and Otto Klein?"

"Precisely. I am now quite certain that he is the murderer of Mrs Court, Mr Cornwell and Mr Groat. For him, it would have been a simple matter to disguise himself and engage Mr Groat in conversation within the club, while he waited for an opportune moment to kill him and escape. Possibly he returned later, having resumed his normal appearance. This killing strikes me as a rather desperate measure however, so it could be concluded that, having discovered Mr Groat's true identity as an agent of Mycroft's department, it was imperative to silence him quickly. Once more, I am forced to the conclusion that the spy ring intends to strike soon. I have omitted of course, in my assessment of Klein's recent crimes, the murderous attempt upon ourselves at the Resurrection Church Hall and the murder of Mr Morton Coleridge."

"You believe that he was murdered, also?"

"I have said as much, but we shall see if evidence to that effect presents itself."

From there the conversation drifted elsewhere, and then we smoked in silence for a while. It was quite late when the door-bell rang, and as we had heard no sound from Mrs Hudson's quarters for some time, Holmes quickly descended the stairs to answer the summons himself.

I rose as he re-entered the room, with a yellow envelope that he had already ripped open. A faint smile adorned his face as he explained.

"It is the expected reply from Gregson. We will see our client at ten o'clock tomorrow morning."

We retired for the night, shortly afterwards. Next morning Holmes seemed rather subdued. I surmised that he was still much concerned with our welfare and the question of our adversary's purpose.

Breakfast was quickly over, and we set out. We procured a hansom without difficulty and arrived early at Scotland Yard, to find that Inspector Gregson was already waiting near the entrance in conversation with a burly constable.

"This is Constable Turley," he said after greetings had been exchanged. "I regret that I cannot be with you gentlemen this morning, but the constable will escort you to the cell of Mr Josiah Endicott and remain present until the interview is over."

Gregson then took his leave, striding urgently out into the street, while our escort guided us down one of the bleak olive-painted corridors until we were confronted with a heavy door. When we had passed through this, he took out a key and opened the fourth of six barred cells. Our client sat in the dark and gloomy interior, and rose to meet us with a relieved expression.

"Mr Holmes! Doctor Watson! Thank God you have come." In the poor light, I saw that the half-healed wounds on his face glistened. "They believe that I killed Mrs Court, one of the victims that I was investigating. Please tell them that I am innocent."

"I can only state that you are innocent as far as we are aware," Holmes answered, "until we are able to do so conclusively. Kindly inform us as to your whereabouts on the day of Mrs Court's death."

He glanced at Constable Turley, before lowering his voice. "During my brief time as an enquiry agent I managed to establish a small circle of informers. That is why I could not divulge my activities at that time to the official force. As you must be aware yourself, to do so would bring the informer's usefulness to an end, and Scotland Yard would demand his assistance without payment."

Holmes nodded. "Pray tell me the name of this man, and I will do my utmost to secure your release."

"It is a beggar, Micah Clowry," Mr Endicott whispered. "He rarely leaves Whitechapel and knows all that occurs there. A collision between a landau and a brougham obliged us to change our venue."

"I know him. He has been of assistance to me also, on occasion. I will attempt to find him this afternoon."

Our client was effusive in his thanks, and little more of any consequence was said before we left. Constable Turley wore a disappointed look, from which I concluded that he had overheard little.

"I am sorry for the man," I remarked as we waited for a cab, "but I cannot see that the testimony of a beggar will make a difference to his unfortunate situation."

"We will see what can be done," Holmes said absently.

We spoke no more until we were again settled in our lodgings. Holmes declined luncheon in favour of a pot of strong coffee, and left abruptly before I had finished my dessert. When Mrs Hudson had cleared away and ensured that I wanted nothing more, I sat before the fire and smoked contentedly. After a while I resumed my perusal of an article in *The Lancet* regarding an outbreak of yellow fever in a region of the African continent where it was hitherto unknown, before lowering it slowly as I surrendered to sleep.

I was suddenly aware of Holmes shaking my shoulder. "Watson, are you awake?"

A deep sleep indeed, I thought, as I realised that he had entered the room and divested himself of his hat and coat without disturbing me. From my pocket-watch I saw with amazement that I had slept for more than four hours, and dinner would be served before long.

"Were you successful?" I asked as my weariness receded.

"Mr Endicott is a free man, and Gregson is slightly embarrassed. I left here directly for Whitechapel, and found Micah Clowry at one of his usual haunts. Overcoming his initial reluctance, I questioned him closely regarding his meeting with our client on the day of the murder of Mrs Court. It soon came to me that his answers contained facts that he could not have known, had he not met Mr Josiah Endicott, and met him at that time. For example, you will recall that our client mentioned that they witnessed the accidental collision of two carriages during their discussion. Mr Clowry elaborated on the incident to a satisfactory degree, and I confirmed the date from a newspaper report. He also described Mr Endicott, making no mention of his facial injuries. Finally, he gave me the number of an officer of the local constabulary with whom he is familiar, since he regularly moves him on."

"Did Gregson accept this?"

"He has done so. I persuaded Mr Clowry, with the promise of a half-sovereign, to accompany me to the Yard. I questioned him again, in the inspector's presence and with his participation. Gregson eventually summoned the officer who, fortunately, was able to confirm that the two men were in Whitechapel together, on that date. It did not please him, but by the end of the interview Gregson had little choice but to admit his mistake. I imagine Mr Endicott has returned to his rooms, by now."

Holmes' mood was much lightened over dinner, no doubt because of his successful bid to restore our client's liberty. Afterwards I expected to sit to smoke and converse as usual, but he surprised me.

"Watson, it is a beautiful evening. Why, the sun will soon be setting and the stars are clearly visible in the waning light. What do you say, old fellow, to a short invigorating walk. I feel that the exercise would be beneficial to us both."

I was truly taken aback, because my friend rarely took exercise for its own sake. However, I would not have dreamt of discouraging him, and I swiftly retrieved our hats and coats.

"Where have you a mind to go?" I enquired as we left Baker Street.

"The Regent's Park would be appropriate."

We arrived presently, and entered through Marylebone. The flower beds, particularly the rose gardens had, I remembered, been beautiful in full bloom but were now declining. Doubtlessly due to the lateness of the hour, there were few people about. Several lone men and three couples slowly circled the boating lake, while a party of elderly ladies clustered around a bench appeared to be concluding some sort of nature study quest. Holmes' conversation varied, ranging from a newly-discovered animal species in Africa as reported in *The Standard* to news of the development of a horseless carriage that he predicted would one day replace the hansom. Finally, as darkness closed in and the park became progressively empty, I could take no more of his prevaricating.

"Holmes, what are we to do regarding Mr Seth Cornwell's possible connection to the Experience Club?"

"I will consider this and tell you my conclusions over breakfast. But there is something else that bothers you, Watson, I feel it. Pray elaborate."

I glanced at an imposing statue before I replied. "I also know you well by this time, Holmes. You rarely indulge in any exercise, without reason or purpose."

"That, I think, is well established."

"So why did you suddenly decide upon this evening walk? That is not like you."

At once he was like a man discussing the most inconsequential and frivolous of topics. "My dear fellow, you really should not concern yourself. I merely sought to ascertain whether our friends at the Experience Club are having us followed, since they seem so keen to work towards our destruction."

His calmness, not for the first time, alarmed me. "And are they?"

"Not at all."

"Could not our walking outdoors after dark provide them with an opportunity to make another attempt on our lives?"

"I consider that most unlikely. Remember that the two attempts so far, at the Resurrection Church Hall and via the Buddha's head at our lodgings, have been away from public view. These are people who do their work in secret, as spies are bound to do."

"You are rarely wrong, Holmes. I hope that this time is not to be an exception."

He then dismissed the subject, and began a discourse on some species of flora that are unique to South America. He had barely finished by the time we returned to Baker Street through gaslit streets, and after enjoying a glass of vintage port together we wished each other good night.

Holmes made no mention of the matter concerning Mr Seth Cornwell, throughout breakfast.

"Have you decided how we shall proceed, in our efforts to establish a connection between him and the other victims," I enquired again after reminding my friend that he had promised to share his conclusions.

He finished the last of his toast and pushed away his empty coffee-cup. "I have. On reflection it seemed that Mr Cornwell's most likely connection would be with Mr Jude Groat, who was a member of the security service. Possibly they met, however briefly, during some high-level investigation of the official force."

"I recall that Mr Endicott implied that Mr Cornwell had conducted his investigations from Scotland Yard, for many years."

"Indeed. That is why I rose while you still slept, Watson, and despatched a telegram to Inspector Gregson asking him to tell us what he can of Mr Cornwell's career. There are many inspectors at the Yard, so it could be that Gregson has never seen or heard of him, but I should think he could discover something from the records or from someone who knew Mr Cornwell. I expect an answer within the next few hours."

As it was, no answer came. Shortly after luncheon I asked my friend how he proposed to continue, and he had hardly replaced his pipe in the rack when the chimes of the door-bell forestalled his reply.

"Gregson", he said confidently on hearing the murmured conversation with Mrs Hudson. "Now we may learn something."

The inspector entered and Holmes ordered tea. When we were all seated our landlady reappeared with a tray, and we drank in silence. The pot was empty when we finally began our discussion.

"I appreciate your calling, Gregson, rather than answering my message. Is there anything you have to tell us?"

"I would not have considered such an enquiry for a moment, had you not been of assistance to myself and my colleagues in the past. You understand, Mr Holmes, that a Scotland Yard Inspector's records are of a confidential nature." He looked straight at my friend, who nodded. "But I have looked into those of Inspector Cornwell and discovered that what you ask is not, strictly speaking, police business. You enquired after any link between him and the Experience Club in Pall Mall and, as it happens, there is brief mention of the place."

"Capital. Pray continue."

"The reason I say that this really does not concern the official force," Gregson said, "is because Inspector Cornwell visited the Experience Club for no other reason than to see it with a view to becoming a member, rather than in the course of an investigation. He was recommended by a long-established member, a friend called Henry Willard, since deceased. Apparently the inspector decided that the club was not to his taste since, as far as is known, he never went there again."

"Did the record mention anyone he might have met there? Mr Vern Fuller or Colonel Tomkins, for example?"

"Indeed it did. Inspector Cornwell had developed a considerable ability to define men's true nature over the years, and he noted that Mr Fuller was unlikely to be trustworthy."

"Discernment, indeed," I remarked.

"There is one more thing that may be relevant. Regarding the Experience Club, a report was received today. It will be in every newspaper by this evening, so nothing is lost by informing you now."

Holmes and I sat forward in our chairs attentively.

"It seems," Inspector Gregson continued without expression in his voice, "that a gentlemen whose connection with the club has been established, left London on the steamship *Der Drache* in the early hours of this morning.

Shortly after clearing the Thames, he fell overboard. I understand that his body has not yet been recovered."

Gregson left soon after, leaving Holmes and I reflecting upon his revelations.

"Who do you think the dead man could be?" I asked to break the silence.

"Obviously one of our three German spies, considering his choice of vessel to use in his escape. Or there may be others who are as yet unknown to us."

"Escape? Is that what you believe?"

"I do. The purpose of the spy ring cannot have been fulfilled as yet. We will most likely find that the body, should it be found, is that of Otto Klein, their assassin whose work is probably considered to be over for the present, hence his attempted return to Germany. I recall noticing that the Experience Club was under observation during our visit, and that suggests only one possibility."

"Have they killed one of their own, because they fear he has been recognised?"

He smiled, briefly. "Oh no, Watson, although I would hesitate to place them above such an act. I see brother Mycroft's hand in this."

"Would he order a man killed, out of hand?"

"I see, old fellow, that you do not fully appreciate my brother's position in the government, nor the power that he wields. If his agents have identified Klein as a significant danger to the British public, or to their own colleagues as he has proved himself, I have no doubt that Mycroft would be reluctant to let him leave these shores unpunished. I doubt less that this is the first time that he has been called upon to make such a decision. Ask yourself, if you were identified as a spy in Imperial Germany, what would you expect your fate to be?"

I nodded, finding the prospect distasteful. "Are you quite certain that it could not have been one of the other two?"

"By no means, but it seems that Mr Vern Fuller and Colonel Tomkins have been installed as resident spymasters in this affair, controlling an unknown number of agents, whereas Otto Klein is a professional assassin called in to clear the way for their purpose by eliminating any perceived threat. However, we shall see."

"Inspector Cornwell became a victim of Klein, I would imagine, because his honed skills of detection sensed something amiss during his conversations at the Experience Club. Someone connected with the spy ring must have realised this."

"Most likely," Holmes confirmed. "Any threat to their objective, or even the suspicion of a threat, would be dealt with ruthlessly. But, we now have our connection. Mr Endicott was correct in his assumption that all three murders were linked, committed by the same person or group and towards the same end."

Nor was that the end of the killings that day. Shortly after dinner we were to discover a further fatality.

Holmes and I sat opposite each other, around the fireplace. We each held an evening edition before our faces as the smoke from our pipes swirled towards the ceiling. From time to time I would hear him murmur, either from satisfaction that some prediction had proved to be true, or because (I supposed) his advice to one of the Scotland Yard inspectors, based on logic and deduction, had assisted the official force.

We continued in companionable silence, as we have for more evenings that I care to remember, when our peace was shattered by his sudden exclamation.

"Watson! Are you reading *The Evening News?*"

"No, I am less than halfway through *The Standard.* Have you found something of interest?"

"Is there a report there of a murder in Camberwell?"

"I have seen no such article."

"That is probably because this paper is a later edition. There is a photographic image here that we should both recognise."

I rose and went over to him. He held the newspaper at an angle that allowed me to see the picture.

"It is Mr Vern Fuller!" I cried, shocked. "What has happened to him?"

"According to this report, he was struck by a passing carriage. As you see, he is quite dead. Inspector Walker believes it was an accident."

"Yet the carriage drove on?"

"Indeed. If we can procure a hansom quickly, we may be in time to examine the body before it is removed."

In that we were fortunate. No sooner had we put on our hats and coats and left our lodgings, than a cab appeared in the fading light.

"You do not believe this to be accidental?" I ventured as we approached Camberwell along a dark and leafy lane with few houses.

"We will see what the evidence has to tell us."

"If Mr Vern Fuller was murdered, who could be responsible?" I lowered my voice. "Not Mycroft, surely?"

"I am inclined to believe that my brother has set his people to watch the Experience Club, infiltrate it even, in order to determine the spy ring's intentions," he replied surprisingly, in his normal tone. Then I recalled that he had shouted our destination to the driver with exaggerated loudness, and concluded that the man was deaf.

"Then, assuming that it was not an accident, does that not leave only Mr Fuller's own people to be considered?"

"I have said that such an action would not surprise me. With men such as these their objective is paramount, meaning that anything or anyone threatening it is considered instantly disposable. If Mr Fuller unwittingly became an impediment to their scheme, he would have been dealt with. As the appearance of an accident has been maintained, the official force are less likely to search for a perpetrator."

"But what could he have done, to place himself in such a dangerous position?"

Holmes shrugged. "We will probably never discover that, but it would take no more than a careless word in the wrong company, or a thoughtless act that might arouse suspicion. Much like the situation that brought about the end of Inspector Cornwell, I would think."

I was about to comment on the outrageous concept of killing one's own comrades, when the hansom drew to a halt. Two uniformed officers stood around a prostrate form. They appeared clearly subordinate to a young fellow in a frock coat.

As we alighted he turned and stared at us enquiringly, and I had the impression that we were about to be dismissed. In the poor light he looked very youthful to have attained his position at the Yard.

Then his expression changed. "Mr Sherlock Holmes? Doctor Watson?"

"Good evening, Inspector," my friend replied. "I hope you will permit us to delay you sufficiently for us to conduct an examination of the body, in connection with a current enquiry."

"I am pleased to meet you gentlemen. We have been here for some hours, for I was called from another case. Inspector Lestrade has often told me of the considerable assistance that you have afforded him and some of his colleagues, on occasion. He has even stated, Mr Holmes, that your skill rivals his own at times."

"Lestrade is most kind," Holmes said with a straight face. "But it is in fact Inspector Gregson who we have conferred with in the course of this enquiry."

Inspector Walker nodded. "I cannot see that there is much for you here, however. These officers stood guard after the accident was reported, until I was summoned. They were able to resist the interference of people from the newspapers.

This man was struck by a passing hansom or coach that failed to stop. With no witnesses it will be difficult to trace the carriage, but we will do what we can. By all means conduct your own inspection."

Holmes thanked him and the three of us knelt by the corpse. The constables moved away to give us room, their eyes occasionally searching the deserted street and its row of shops.

"It would seem," said the inspector, "that the coach struck him as he crossed the road, causing him to hit the wall and rebound. There are bloody traces on the brickwork."

Holmes looked up at the wall before turning the body slightly. "So it would appear, and yet there is no brick dust or any indication of the impact on the dead man's clothes. Suppose for a moment that he was forced to stand in the path of the coach to absorb the force of the collision which propelled him forward, before his blood was daubed on the wall to distort what actually occurred." He pointed to a patch of mud a few feet away, across which something heavy had clearly been dragged.

"That seems possible. But how on earth could he have been induced to remain still, as the horses bore down on him?"

Something occurred to me immediately. I slid the sleeve of the dead man's evening coat up his arm and removed the cuff-link to roll back his shirt-sleeve. Finding nothing, I repeated this on the other arm. "Holmes!"

My friend peered, with the aid of his dark lantern, at the revealed flesh. I saw that my supposition was correct.

"Those marks, Inspector, are from an injection by means of a hypodermic syringe. Doubtlessly, a strong sedative was applied. I doubt if he was aware of the danger."

"I see. You believe then, that he was afterwards repositioned and the blood-marks applied to the wall, to give the impression that he was attempting to cross the road as the collision occurred?"

"A disguised execution," I suggested.

"I merely offer my observations and conclusions as an alternative possibility," My friend said evenly. I saw that he tried not to discourage Inspector Walker, who was clearly new to his post. "I have found it instructive to always take account of surroundings and other details, rather than to accept situations as they appear at first sight. We have learned what we can here, I think, assuming that you have already searched the corpse's clothing?"

"It contained only a handkerchief, a wallet that was empty but for two five-pound notes, and a card stuck in the lining of one of the pockets."

"But nothing to identify the man?"

The Scotland Yard detective shook his head. "There was nothing more."

"I would like to examine the card, if you would be so kind."

It was quickly produced, and Holmes gave it a scant look after turning it over in his hand. "Thank you, Inspector."

"You can learn nothing from it?"

Holmes smiled briefly. "Only that it advertises a paint factory in Hampstead Heath."

"Very well, then. I will have the body removed to the mortuary."

"Doctor Watson and myself wish you success in your pursuit of the answer to this extraordinary killing. Good-night, Inspector."

At Holmes' request, the hansom had waited. We were clear of Camberwell, and passing a barn that stood in darkness along a lane set amid extensive fields, when I attempted to remonstrate with my friend.

"Holmes, I would have thought you could have provided the Inspector with a measure of assistance."

"What would you have had me disclose?"

"Surely, the corpse's name and connection with the Experience Club would have helped."

"Are you not forgetting the secret nature of this affair, old friend? Did not Brother Mycroft attempt to discourage us? Also, and I confess to considering this foremost, to have more Scotland Yarders as potential hindrances to our investigation can be of no advantage. Inspector Walker will make his own way through the case and draw his own conclusions in the course of time. By then, I have every hope that we will have solved it."

"So," I said when we were once more safely ensconced in our lodgings, "we now know the fate of Mr Vern Fuller. I am wondering how many at the Experience Club are aware of the incident."

"That we will ascertain in the morning," Holmes replied as he extinguished his pipe, "but for now I will suggest that we have a new direction for our enquiry, before wishing you good-night."

He retired to his room immediately, leaving me wondering as to his meaning.

For some reason, I slept little that night. Bleary-eyed, I sat through breakfast hardly conscious of what I ate. Holmes consumed his kippers with his usual indifference, his eagerness to proceed with our enquiry ill-concealed.

"Come, Watson," he said as he rose from the table, "we must ascertain the situation at the Experience Club before venturing further."

The hansom deposited us in Pall Mall with little delay, and we approached the double doors as before. The same elderly steward informed us that neither Mr Vern Fuller or Colonel Tomkins were available. When Holmes pressed him, he reluctantly disclosed that both members had left the club without explanation, but that this was not unusual.

"Evidently," my friend observed as we left, "news of Mr Fuller's death has not reached all the members yet."

"And Colonel Tomkins is missing also. Is it possible that his body too, lies undiscovered somewhere?"

"Possible yes, but I do not consider it likely. I formed the impression that Colonel Tomkins was the senior of the two within the organisation, which means that it could have been he who disposed of his comrade if he was so ordered. The fact that the Colonel is not available may mean that he has hidden himself somewhere as the date for the fulfilment of their purpose draws near."

I saw that my friend was considering how to proceed, as I enquired: "Holmes, last night you indicated that you have a new direction in mind for our investigation."

"Indeed," he replied. "But I see a hansom approaching. On our return to Baker Street I must consult my index. After that I will explain all."

During the journey, he sat with a thoughtful expression and said little. On entering our sitting-room he threw off his hat and coat and immediately selected several scrapbooks, feverishly scanning the pages and rejecting one after another.

I sat in my usual chair, waiting to be of help if I could. More than twenty minutes passed with the discarded papers littering the carpet, when my friend suddenly became still. "Aha!"

"You have found what you were seeking?"

"I have. Look at this, Watson."

He produced a photographic picture of a tall, well-dressed man about to enter a courtyard through iron gates.

I scrutinised the image, shaking my head. "Who is this?"

"Of course," he put a hand to his forehead, "that affair took place shortly after your marriage. What am I thinking of?"

"Holmes, you are speaking in riddles."

"Allow me to apologise, old fellow. This is Sir James Stickleford, whose company manufactures metal goods. Everything from safety pins to gun barrels, I'm told. He received his knighthood for his contribution to rearming our forces engaged in foreign wars and in the colonies. Some years ago an attempt was made to blackmail him under threat of a scandal that would have shaken the empire, but I was able to deduce the source and the scoundrels were apprehended. A trifling problem really, but Sir James was endlessly grateful. I refused payment, whereupon he made it clear that he would always be available to assist me in any way at all times. He is a charming fellow, and I am certain that he will accede to a small request."

"What have you in mind?"

"Simply a list of his current competitors."

I frowned. "How will that advance our investigation?"

"Patience, Watson." He scribbled on a telegram form and tore it from the pad. "Is our page boy in attendance today?"

"I believe so. Mrs Hudson will be serving him luncheon, at this hour."

"As she will us, very soon. But for now, be a good fellow and, at the risk of disturbing his meal, call him up to the landing. If you would give him this message and these coins I would be much obliged."

I complied of course, and the young man set off for the nearest Post Office at once. I returned to our room to find Holmes sitting back in his chair blowing smoke rings at the ceiling. He put aside his clay pipe as I settled myself opposite.

"I will now attempt to satisfy your curiosity," he said. "I anticipate that we will be here for most of the afternoon, but an answer to my message will surely be here not long after. You see, I have asked Sir James to enlighten me as to who are the manufacturers of that Buddha's head which still resides over there in the corner, or else to tell me of any new producers of such goods. From there we may be able to trace the origin of that bauble, and the whereabouts of whoever purchased it."

"He whose intention was to poison you?"

"Precisely. It will be a pleasure to make his acquaintance. I recommend that we each pack a clean collar, cuffs and a toothbrush, since it is likely that we shall be travelling some distance before long."

This we did, although I failed to understand fully Holmes' intended method of procedure.

We had no sooner completed this task than our dear landlady arrived with our luncheon. Holmes' eyes glittered with enthusiasm at the prospect of this new direction, his preoccupation was such that I was surprised when he announced that Mrs Hudson's curried fowl had never before tasted so good.

Chapter 8 – Mendells Lodge

The answering telegram from Sir James arrived far sooner than either Holmes or myself had expected. My friend had returned to his index, I suspect in an attempt to tidy it, while I wrote up notes on the progress of some of my patients. The peal of the door-bell stilled us both, and we looked at each other as Mrs Hudson answered. Immediately after, we heard her footsteps upon the stairs.

Holmes consulted his pocket-watch. "Sir James was prompt with his reply, for it is not yet four o'clock. It may be that we can depart on the late afternoon train."

He rose and went to answer the knock on our door, accepting the telegram and conducting a brief discussion with our landlady. I assumed this was to inform her of our forthcoming absence, since she said little in response except to enquire whether she should prepare dinner.

As she returned to her quarters, he unfolded the telegram and studied it for a moment before addressing me.

"Watson, kindly consult my Bradshaws for the next train to Hernesgrove, in the West Midlands. I recall that the village is about six miles south of Stratford-upon-Avon."

I turned the pages quickly. "The last train departs from Paddington at 4:50. If we are to catch it, we have no time to lose."

As I replaced the volume, he put on his hat and coat and handed me mine. We quickly retrieved our overnight travelling bags and descended the stairs. I was first in Baker Street, Holmes having paused to shout to Mrs Hudson, and we were most fortunate in that a passing hansom stopped for us at my signal.

"That was convenient, Holmes," I remarked as we took our seats.

"Indeed." He shouted our destination, promising the driver an extra half-sovereign if we arrived in time for the train. The horse took on a fair pace, faltering but once when a laden cart driven by a surly-looking rough emerged from a side-street at what I considered to be an irresponsible speed. As it was, we arrived at Paddington Station with enough time to spare for Holmes to purchase the tickets before our train hurtled into view amid clouds of smoke and screeching brakes. There were few other passengers, and we experienced no difficulty in securing a smoker to ourselves.

"Now that we are settled," I said as the train gathered speed, quickly leaving the station behind, "perhaps you would care to confide in me. You have not yet explained Sir James' response to your request. I presume you have identified this place Hernesgrove as a possible stronghold of our adversaries?"

"I have, since almost all the other producers of classical likenesses in metal are well-known and long established. Sir James pointed out that, of the two exceptions, our present destination is the most likely to have manufactured the Buddha's head."

I took out my pipe, and he did likewise. "What of the remaining exception?"

"That is a new concern that trades in the north of Scotland, mostly in images in lead. I understand that their speciality is characters from the traditional Greek legends."

"What then, are we to expect in Hernesgrove?"

"Apparently, the late Lord Keltingham left no heirs, and so his estate, Mendells Lodge, has been left unattended for some years while solicitors and others attempt to trace distant relatives who have long since lived abroad. Eventually, one such elderly man was discovered in Australia, and he has given authority for the place to be rented out. For the last six months the house has been partially occupied, together with the out-buildings, by a small concern manufacturing articles such as that sent to me."

I blew out a cloud of smoke, which swirled above us as his had done. "Obviously then, you believe that this is a concealment, that the true nature of this enterprise somehow connects with the spy ring within the Experience Club?"

"Either that, or they simply sold the Buddha to whoever installed the poison before sending it on. When we have determined which of these is the truth, we will know how to proceed."

We smoked for a while in silence, watching the changing scene before us. The buildings of the city had long since given way to open countryside, green fields and small forests eager for the coming summer. Villages, comprising little more than a church, an inn or two and rows of shops and cottages sped by, until the light began to fade as we drew nearer to our destination.

I had become drowsy, and had to fight to remain awake, although Holmes seemed unaffected by the lulling motion of the train and the warmth of our compartment, by the time we arrived in the tiny country station. It appeared to be run by a fat and cheerful fellow who was everything from porter to station master. He took our tickets and informed us that the best inn that the village had to offer was the Black Bull, less than a quarter of a mile distant.

We thanked him and, with so little luggage, covered the distance easily. The tree-lined lane felt eerie in the darkness, with the occasional gas-lamp casting grotesque shadows. At its end began a long and narrow street of closed shops and thatched cottages, some of which were in darkness, interrupted by an ancient church. Across the street the Black Bull stood out, not only because of its newly-whitewashed exterior, but because of the sounds of merriment from within.

Some of the noise abated as we entered, as local farmers and herdsmen paused in their drinking to scrutinize us. The landlord seemed pleasant enough, and was pleased to show us two clean and adequate rooms atop a creaking staircase. I believe that my friend would have foregone supper in favour of an early night, had I not insisted. Nevertheless, he did justice to his steak and kidney pie as I did to mine. These we washed down with a pint each of the landlord's best ale, before bidding him good night and retiring.

I slept dreamlessly, and unexpectedly well, which I attributed to the quiet which descended after closing-time and the clear country air. I heard nothing of Holmes until we met at the head of the stairs on our way to breakfast.

"Did you sleep well, Watson?" He enquired as we descended.

"Exceedingly so."

"I am glad to hear it, since today promises to demand much of our energy. First I must speak to the landlord, since his local knowledge will be most useful."

"We appear to be the only guests," I remarked as we sat down at one of the tables in the small dining-room. "Also, it seems that the landlord and his wife employ no servants or helpers."

"I imagine that the customers we saw last night are all local folk, and probably the only regulars. Strangers probably visit here rarely. You will have observed the suspicious glances we received as we entered the premises."

At that moment, the landlord appeared.

"Good morning, gentlemen. I trust you slept well?"

We affirmed that we did.

"Would you care to breakfast on locally reared ham, together with eggs from our own hens?"

That suggestion, to both of us, was most acceptable.

A large pot of coffee was produced while we waited, but the man reappeared remarkably quickly with two plates of steaming food.

"Thank you, landlord," said Holmes. "I wonder if you, as a local man, could advise us. My friend and I are conducting a survey for the Land Commission, involving visits to mansions and grand houses that have fallen into disrepair. It has come to our attention that such a structure, known as Mendells Lodge, is situated nearby. We would be grateful for any information you could supply regarding this building, for we have discovered that little is known, officially."

The man nodded, and lowered his serving tray. Adopting a thoughtful expression, he addressed both of us.

"Well, I'll tell you what I can, gentlemen. The place was the home of Lord Keltingham for many years. He was still a young man when Lady Keltingham died in a local influenza epidemic, causing him to become a recluse for a while. Then suddenly he was seen about the village again, and there was talk of him bringing in ladies all the way from Stratford and Birmingham. Certainly he was known to have entertained quite a few at Mendells Lodge before he died, peacefully in his bed it is said. The law people could trace no heir, I have heard, except for a distant relative in Australia. This person has had the place rented out and I've been told that part of the property is now used as some sort of factory." He paused, scratching his head. "I don't rightly see that there is much more to tell."

"Your information is most valuable," Holmes assured him. "Our thanks to you."

The man bowed his head in acknowledgement and left us to our meal. He returned shortly and took our plates, replacing the coffee pot at the same time.

"I think, Watson, we will take a turn around the district today," Holmes decided when our cups were empty once more. "I have a mind to see what can be learned at Mendells Lodge."

So it was that we set out shortly after. An elderly fellow, obviously a retired farmer Holmes deduced, sat smoking on a bench near the village green and was good enough to supply us with directions. He estimated the distance to Mendells Lodge to be half a mile but, after arriving by way of a long narrow lane which brought us to the road, I was certain that we had walked a full mile at least.

"The house is imposing, but has certainly seen better days," Holmes observed as we passed the ornamental gates. "The low structures in the courtyard and at the side of the building appear to have once been stables and were probably used for storage but, judging by the smoke and the noise which is discernible even from this distance, they have been given over to industrial use. I have no doubt that baubles such as the Buddha's head are manufactured here as the apparent purpose of the place, but I wonder at the true reason for it all. I think, Watson, that we will visit here again to see whether things are as they seem."

"You are thinking, no doubt, of an excursion after dark?"

"Quite so. But now let us walk a little further before we turn back, so that it does not appear that to observe the house was the object of our presence here. I saw the glint of sunlight on something in that direction, which could mean that passers-by are watched by means of field-glasses."

We continued along the road and entered the surrounding forest. It was cool beneath the trees and we soon found a fallen trunk on which to sit and smoke. After twenty minutes had passed, according to my pocket-watch, we retraced our steps. As we came upon Mendells Lodge again, we never once looked in that direction.

At luncheon, Holmes surprised me by asking the landlord: "By any chance, was there an enquiry after us this morning, during our absence?"

The man clapped a hand to his brow. "My sincere apologies, sir. I had meant to mention it but it somehow slipped my mind. A gentleman did approach me as I prepared the tables for luncheon. He described you and asked your names, saying he was unsure whether you were old friends from his schooldays."

A brief look of satisfaction passed over my friend's face. "Was he a small man, with a scar on his right cheek?"

"Oh no, sir. He was fairly tall, but not as tall as yourself, thin-faced and balding at the front of his head."

"Ah yes. I doubt if he will call again, but should he do so at a time when we are here, pray call us at once."

"Of course, sir." The landlord's tone was still apologetic. "Is the meal to your liking?"

"The stew is excellent," Holmes said, and I concurred.

More customers arrived, both in the bar-room and seeking a meal. The landlord shouted for his wife's assistance and left us to serve them.

When we were alone, save for the occupants of two tables near the entrance, I put down my cutlery and conferred with Holmes in a low voice.

"Who were you expecting to ask after us? The local official force, perhaps? Could Gregson or one of his colleagues have followed us here?"

He laughed, to my embarrassment. "My dear fellow, why should any of those be interested in us? No, whoever the enquirer was, you can be certain that his intentions were not to our benefit. You realised of course that we were followed, during our walk to Mendells Lodge?"

"Surely not!" I retorted. "I saw no one."

"But I did. I noticed a man in tweeds, with a monocle worn over his left eye, twice as we sought the house and once as we returned. Oh, do not let your lack of observation worry you, Watson, at least on this occasion. These people are no amateurs, which means that their purpose is one that is vital to their masters. They would not send such skilled agents, otherwise."

"But Holmes, we are in deadly danger. They knew we were staying here, and our names."

He shook his head. "Do not concern yourself overmuch. The landlord did not say that he was asked about us by name, and in any case the fictitious ones we gave him would be meaningless to them. The sudden appearance of any strangers hereabouts would be bound to arouse the interest, if not the suspicion, of our adversaries. I am inclined to think that all newcomers are treated similarly, as a routine precaution. Doubtlessly, we will see before long."

"Are we to pursue things further then, this afternoon?"

"Not at all!" His expression lightened suddenly. "I suggest we spend the time walking in a leisurely fashion around this charming village. It may be to our advantage to get to know the area better. Then, after the rainbow trout that the landlord is pleased to advertise on his blackboard in the bar-room, we will see if we can advance our enquiries further."

We did indeed walk around enjoying the village and the countryside, until dinner. Holmes was particularly interested in the ancient stocks outside a decaying building that could once have been a courthouse. They would have been the instrument of punishment, centuries before, of minor offenders, while the so-called 'hangman's tree', according to a volume in the local library, ended the lives of highwaymen and other serious wrongdoers.

"The village must have been much larger, in past times," I remarked.

"Indeed. Before the main highway was adopted this was a direct trading route for merchants from the south. They would have been travelling to Birmingham most likely, as the greatest centre of commerce in the land."

"Have we been followed since luncheon?" I asked him, abruptly changing the subject.

"No. They may have lost interest in us, thinking that we are no threat to them, or be waiting for us to take some action."

"Let us hope that we are not seen tonight."

"Come, Watson, we have found ourselves in similar situations before now. We will however, take great care."

Dinner at the inn took longer than before, with the landlord serving many more diners. When it was over we returned to our rooms for our hats and coats, which fortunately were of dark colours. Daylight was failing as we set off in the direction of Mendells Lodge, and had faded completely by the time we arrived.

"The gates are locked, but the fence should present little difficulty." Holmes adjusted his ear-flapped travelling cap and took hold of a thick wooden post. "It was constructed to contain beasts, not to serve as an obstacle against intruders."

He seemed to find footholds easily and hoisted himself upwards, disappearing over the top as the moon shone briefly from between banks of cloud. I followed, but less gracefully than he and with less agility. When we stood inside the fence we immediately concealed ourselves behind a large beech, carefully searching our surroundings for signs of human presence.

"Observe the area carefully," he whispered. "There will certainly be guards. We must avoid them at all costs, since if we are confronted there is no choice but to render them harmless if that is possible. Their subsequent discovery would ensure that any hope of secrecy would be lost, and our task made all the more difficult."

He had no sooner said this before the snapping of a twig underfoot caused us to draw deeper into the shadow of the beech. For a moment nothing disturbed the stillness, and then the shape of a thick-set man emerged from the gloom. We froze, as motionless as statues, and I held my breath until he passed. In a moment he was out of our sight.

"We are fortunate in that they are not using dogs," Holmes said in a tone that I hardly heard. "But there will be other guards."

Slowly and carefully, we advanced towards the buildings. These seemed as they had appeared on our earlier visit, but with lights shining from within amidst the clamour of machines and voices. We concealed ourselves behind a row of bushes, away from the glare of the light but within the shadow of the house. Presently someone out of our sight barked harsh orders, and a party of running men entered the sheds. After a short while another group emerged and walked wearily towards the house.

"A change of shift," Holmes whispered.

"I would swear that the orders were shouted by Colonel Tomkins."

"Or someone else with a military voice."

We observed the huts for some time, twice becoming silent and still as guards, now clearly seen to be armed, appeared nearby. The largest of the sheds emitted light that shone much brighter than the rest, and much of the noise and the shouting seemed to originate there. I could see that this interested Holmes, but also that he might be somewhat perplexed. I estimated that two hours had passed, with no sign of further activity or change.

"I think we will leave now, Watson. Be ready to retreat into concealment at any moment."

He rose and moved away silently and I followed. As we approached the trees near the fence a guard came into sight and we were immediately still. I was about to whisper to Holmes but he gripped my arm to indicate the need for silence, and we remained unmoving. The guard continued to peer in our direction, seemingly uncertain as to what had attracted his attention. Moments passed, and we strained to hold our breath. The guard remained as he was for what seemed like an hour, then his motion was suddenly resumed. We allowed time for him to get well out of earshot, in case he should be wily enough to continue watching from the trees, before moving slowly towards the fence. Holmes was over it in seconds, pausing to assist me as I searched for a handhold. We saw not a soul during our return to the inn, and Holmes assured me that we were no longer followed.

Next morning brought torrential rain, with no break in the heavy dark clouds. The grim scene was reflected in my friend's expression, so that he said little as we breakfasted.

"We can but hope for an end, or at least for a lessening, to this inclement weather," He remarked as we smoked our first pipes of the day after our plates had been cleared away. "I am anxious to learn more about the inhabitants of Mendells Lodge."

Shortly after, he retreated to his room. I saw him at luncheon and his mood was unchanged, as was the weather, but as the hour for dinner approached the sky began to clear. The evening promised to display what I think of as one of Nature's apologies, a beautiful sunset as if the day had been pleasant. Having grown tired of reading in my room, I was glad to see that Holmes was more companionable, and eager to resume our investigation. As we ate, our plans were made.

After darkness had fallen we set out once again. As we approached Mendells Lodge it was at once clear that the situation had altered. We stepped back from the road as several carts thundered past, their drivers urging the horses to greater speed. From the concealment of thick bushes we watched as more followed, ghost-like in the moonlight. Finally the road was quiet again, and I rose, only to be immediately pulled back to my former position by Holmes.

"Not yet, Watson," he hissed. "I hear more coming."

We remained crouched there for another minute, according to my estimate, and then a much larger vehicle appeared. Pulled by six horses it must have been at least twenty feet long, and carrying a broad wooden case that filled almost its entire length. The driver was a cruel man, continually cursing the poor beasts and using his whip excessively. It rattled and bumped along the uneven road, and then was gone.

When all sound had ceased, Holmes rose cautiously. I followed and we stood statue-still, listening for anyone approaching on foot. After a few moments an owl hooted from somewhere deep in the trees, and something scuttled quickly away among the bushes, but there was no other sound.

"Do you hear anything more, Holmes?" I asked.

In the faint light of the moon, I saw him shake his head. "There is nothing. I believe they have abandoned the place."

We trudged on for a little while, until the dark shape of the house appeared. A single light remained, shining from a ground floor window. The sheds and other out-buildings were in darkness. We saw at once that it was unnecessary to climb the fence, for the gates had been left open.

"There is still someone there," I observed.

"Guards also, perhaps. Keep your weapon handy, and move with caution as before."

Holmes took the lead and we moved from bush to bush, from tree to tree. As we neared the courtyard without encountering guards or seeing any sign of remaining occupancy, he gripped my arm and we immediately took shelter. The explanation for his action became obvious as a giant of a man came into our view, leading two restless horses.

A spark of moonlight reflected from their bridles and the man cursed the unruliness of the beasts, looking around him as if awaiting a signal or the arrival of a companion. Shortly afterwards the light in the house was extinguished before two more men appeared, one half-crawling as the other followed administering brutal kicks.

"Do not move, Watson." Holmes had sensed my outrage at this treatment, and his whisper was urgent. I forced myself to watch.

The scene darkened as the moon passed behind a drifting cloud. We heard angry shouts in guttural German from the tormentor, as the other received a further kick and cried out in pain. The moon reappeared, and now we could see its dull glint on the barrel of a pistol. I turned to my friend.

"Holmes, the man with the gun is…..!"

"Colonel Tomkins," he finished. "I had wondered at his place in all this."

Then our attention was riveted on the colonel, for he shot the man prone before him twice in the head. He stepped smartly away, probably to avoid the spreading blood, before marching stiffly and unconcernedly to where his comrade held the horses. He mounted he nearest beast and held the reins of the other while, at a gesture, his companion approached the body and dragged it into the bushes.

Colonel Tomkins barked an order and the other man retrieved the reins of his horse and mounted. The hooves of the beasts clattered and echoed on the paved courtyard as they were spurred into a gallop. In seconds they were gone, and silence returned.

Chapter 9 – Their Purpose Eludes Us

When we were quite sure that the riders had gone, that the last sounds of their horses were muted by distance, we emerged from our concealment.

"Over here, Watson," Holmes directed urgently, "there is a faint chance that the poor fellow might still live."

Ignoring the trail of blood, I rushed with him to the place where the body had been so unceremoniously hidden. In the light of Holmes' dark lantern, I saw at once that the man's head was shattered and that bleeding was extensive.

"I am sorry, Holmes. I am afraid there is no hope."

He looked on silently, his expression as grim as I have ever seen.

"Is this man known to you?" I enquired, because he seemed unusually concerned.

"No, I cannot say that I know who he is. However, I am fairly certain as to *what* he is, or was."

"Someone from Scotland Yard, perhaps?"

"Or one of Mycroft's people. We shall see. I will arrange for his removal later. For now, I think an examination of the house and out-buildings is in order."

With our weapons drawn, we entered the house from the courtyard by the main door. Before long we found oil lamps, which illuminated the interior sufficiently to enable our exploration. The house had certainly been abandoned, and the occupants had exercised great care. Apart from a partial footprint in the trace of soot near a fireplace, they appeared to have left no indication of their presence. When I remarked upon this, Holmes did not disagree.

"As I observed previously, these people are professionals. They are trained to leave no indication as to their identity or their purpose. There are two rooms at ground level that have been occupied, and both have been thoroughly cleaned. Obstacles have been placed on both staircases to prevent access to the upper floors, no doubt because cleaning measures would have been more extensive otherwise. There are no papers or clothing or personal possessions that might have been helpful, which again suggests professional thoroughness. A visit during daylight hours might reveal more, but I think we will leave that to the local constabulary. As for us, we have the sheds and other buildings to examine."

"You intend to contact the official force, then?"

He nodded. "We will return to Baker Street by the early train. Before that I will telegraph Gregson, explaining much that has transpired. Doubtlessly he will inform his local counterparts of the situation and that poor fellow will be removed. An official investigation will ensue, but by then ours will have advanced somewhat. Come, Watson, we must complete our work here before the oil in our lamps is exhausted."

The first three out-buildings yielded very little. Again, our adversaries had removed tools, material and anything that could have provided a clue as to their purpose.

"They have been stringent in their withdrawal arrangements," Holmes observed, "but they could not have removed all the traces of metal dust. It was in these sheds that objects such as the Buddha's head were manufactured, to explain the existence of this place and conceal its true purpose."

"Of which we are still unaware."

"Indeed, but it must be something of consequence. Men are not usually killed because of their interest in the creation of metal decorations and baubles."

In the final structure, the largest of the sheds from where the brightest light had emanated, my friend laid his lamp upon the floor.

"Bring your light over here, Watson, there is something more. Occupying this central space are sizable melting vats, which still retain a little of the warmth from their earlier use." He scooped up a handful of dust. "This also is different. Even to the naked eye and in this poor light, it is apparent that the metal used here was quite unlike that which we discovered in the other buildings. I am inclined to think that the work carried out here was the true objective of Colonel Tomkins and his friends."

"Can we identify its nature?"

"Possibly I could, if we had more time. Otherwise I feel, it would be unwise to draw hasty conclusions. We can be certain from their sudden departure that the work was recently finished, or that they had detected our investigation and feared that we would bring the authorities down upon them."

As the light from our lamps faded, he examined the edges of the interior and the entrance to the shed. The door had been removed and cast carelessly aside, and the door-frame had been deliberately damaged to widen it for the passage of something of much broader dimensions.

"Whatever was transported from here was substantially heavy," Holmes concluded. "The ropes and chains piled outside appear to have been part of a system of pulleys and," he held up his lamp and peered through the waning light, "the large iron hooks affixed to the beams above us suggest this also."

"What can they have created here, Holmes?"

"That, I think, we will most likely discover before many more weeks have passed." He cast a final glance at his surroundings. "But now we will return to the inn. At breakfast I will inform the landlord that we are departing."

The walk back was eerie, and startling when disturbed birds made frantic noises among the trees, but uneventful. To our surprise the landlord was still up and about, explaining that he was a frequent suffer of insomnia. On hearing of our proposed return to the capital, the fellow volunteered to prepare for us an early breakfast soon after first light. After a fitful night, for the memory of the execution constantly interrupted my sleep, I packed my few things and met Holmes downstairs.

"I have checked the local time-table," he informed me when we had eaten and drank to our satisfaction, "so all that remains is to settle with our friend the landlord before we set off." He consulted his pocket-watch. "If we leave the Black Bull in fifteen minutes, we should arrive at the station with time to spare."

And so it proved to be. The landlord seemed excessively delighted as Holmes paid our bill, from which I deduced that a handsome tip had been included. The morning was bright and sunny and the walk pleasant, so that we were both in good spirits as we boarded the early London-bound train. After a revision of our findings as we smoked, we lapsed into a companionable silence. I confess to allowing weariness to overcome me, so that I slept for much of the journey. During my several brief moments of wakefulness, I saw that Holmes stared from the window, unmoving and expressionless.

We had been back in our lodgings for little more than an hour, during which Mrs Hudson had served us mid-afternoon tea and reminded us that dinner would be served on time. I began to suspect that Holmes was searching for some new indication to the whereabouts of Colonel Tomkins or seeking to know his purpose, for he scribbled out two telegrams (one to Gregson and the other to Mycroft, he later explained) expressing such an enquiry in an oblique fashion. Our pageboy had no sooner departed, again bound for the Post Office, than my friend began sorting through his accumulated post, tearing open envelopes and dismissing their contents at an alarming rate. All that awaited my attention were new issues of several medical journals and three letters from old colleagues but, as I put these aside to be perused later, I saw that he had retained but two documents.

"These only are of interest," he announced. "The first is several days old and requests my help in recovering a kidnapped child, but I see from this edition of yesterday's *Standard* that Scotland Yard have excelled themselves in bringing the case to a rapid close already. My faith in Hopkins is justified, it would seem."

"I am exceedingly glad to hear this," I knocked out my pipe in the hearth, "but what of the other document?"

His eyes ran over the paper for a second time. "Now this is something else again. When I am certain that I cannot advance our present case until further information is at hand, I may look into this affair. At the very least, it bears some interest."

He would say nothing more. Regrettably, the replies to his telegrams told us nothing. Colonel Tomkins had vanished and even though Holmes made use of the Irregulars to scour London for the slightest clue, nothing was found. Then another answer was received from Mycroft, revealing only that Colonel Tomkins true identity was Hans Veidermann, known to be a ruthless and experienced agent in the service of the Kaiser.

"Brother Mycroft throws me this morsel either in an attempt to induce me to trouble him less for information, or because he now wishes to encourage our enquiries," Holmes remarked, "which can only mean that his own people are encountering difficulties. Pah! Of what use is this, other than to add the man's true name to my index? For the moment I will pursue this other affair, while hoping for developments."

So it was, that for the next two weeks nothing useful transpired. Holmes buried himself in the curious affair that I have related elsewhere as "The Adventure of the False Aristocrat", which he brought to a satisfactory conclusion at the end of that time, stating that it was disappointingly lacking in original features.

It was soon after that Holmes received a telegram imploring him to come to the assistance of a woman and child trapped in a warehouse in Lambeth. The message explained at length that the pair were being sought by a criminal gang who intended to kill them, in revenge for Inspector Carson's capture and the subsequent execution of their former leader and his brother.

To my amazement Holmes dropped the telegram onto the table, where it came to rest among the remains of his breakfast, and laughed harshly.

"I fail to see what amuses you," I remarked with some curiosity.

After a moment, he recovered himself. "Watson, I have been lured into traps and situations that have threatened my life before, as you well know, but never quite so obviously."

"But this is a cry for help," I paused, attempting to see the situation as he had done. "No, wait - if the woman and child are trapped, how did they send the telegram?"

"Excellent, but that is but one fault in the fabrication. Others include the question of why, even assuming it was possible to send a message, they did not do so first to Scotland Yard. Also, I am familiar with the case, where Carson arrested Ezra Brull for a murder committed during a Post Office raid. I am quite certain that Brull had no brother."

"What do you make of it, then?" I asked, before a thought came to mind. "I have not forgotten the attempt on our lives at Resurrection Church Hall. Could this be another attempt by Colonel Tomkins to remove a threat to his plans?"

"Whatever his intentions may be, it is possible. It struck me as strange, that we have heard nothing of him lately. However, this is a rather amateur inducement as I have said. It could be that the colonel is busy with the final stages of his objective, and has delegated our removal to an underling." He sighed. "Probably a local criminal but not, I am afraid, a very capable fellow."

"Then, having discerned these things, you have decided to ignore the message?" I ventured.

His eyes glittered and he adopted that familiar look that reminded me of a hound, eager for the chase. "Not for the world, old friend, and I hope you will accompany me. If so, ensure that you are armed, as will I."

Less than two hours later, we found ourselves watching the warehouse that the telegram had specified with such urgency, from concealment across a busy street.

"No one has entered or left since we arrived," Holmes observed. "They are probably waiting within."

"Then the trap is set. Has it occurred to you that, once we are inside, they could lock the door and burn the warehouse down?"

He smiled. "Indeed it has, that is why we are loitering here."

"We are not to enter?"

"Of course not, but I fear we may be waiting for some time."

He was correct. I consulted my pocket-watch often within the next two hours, as we stood watching the entrance in silence. A short while later Holmes retreated slightly, moving deeper into the shadows, and I knew that our vigil was over.

"Observe, Watson, but do not speak or move."

The door of the warehouse opened slowly, and a rather pale fellow appeared. He glanced up and down the street before stepping onto the pavement, and was followed by another man and a woman with black hair. They conversed briefly, and then a cab was summoned. The white-faced man and the woman climbed in and the horse set off at a fast trot. The remaining man turned and strode briskly in the opposite direction, soon to pass from our sight.

"A moment more, and then we follow." We hesitated and then left our concealment to take the same path, carefully shielding ourselves by means of other pedestrians. Holmes was expert at this, he used shop windows and other reflective surfaces to keep his quarry in sight while remaining close and invisible in the midst of a crowd. In all the years of my association with him, I had never known his pursuit to be detected.

We drew nearer, because the man we followed had slowed his pace, and Holmes silently held up a hand as a signal that we should do the same. The crowd of passers-by became sparse as we turned into a side street. Our quarry entered a narrow alley and we hesitated again, for it appeared deserted and if we followed we would certainly be seen. Allowing time for the man to gain a short distance, we crossed the carpet of refuse scattered before us.

Tall houses reared up on both sides, causing the alley to appear of less width still. As we emerged into another street I saw the man, now further ahead, look over his shoulder but then continue as before, indicating that he was unfamiliar with our appearance. It seemed safe to continue and Holmes broke into a meaningless conversation, doubtlessly intended to avoid the impression of pursuit.

Then another figure, who must have been waiting out of sight within a gateway ahead, approached quickly. The man we followed stopped, and it became apparent that this was an arranged meeting. Before anything could be said, the newcomer gave a cry of surprise at the sight of us. Our identities were evidently known to him, for he had no hesitation in drawing a pistol and firing frantically. I felt something tear through the sleeve of my coat.

Holmes had clearly anticipated this, for he pushed me against the wall and fired in return. Our attacker dropped his firearm, clutching his chest as a crimson stain spread across his shirt. His companion, who we had followed, produced a revolver but had no opportunity to use it before my friend's second bullet struck him. He sank to his knees, gripping his stomach as blood oozed between his fingers.

"Careful, Watson, you will observe that one of them has retained his grip on his pistol." Holmes took a police whistle from his pocket and blew it continually, and I confess to being surprised at the speed of the response. A young constable appeared from behind us, and quickly approached. He recognised us at once.

"Mr Sherlock Holmes, sir," he said breathlessly. "What has occurred here?"

"We were fired upon by these men, who we suspect are implicated in a serious enquiry that we are pursuing," Holmes explained.

The young fellow nodded. "My beat passes near here, and I heard the reports," He glanced at the bodies. "But look, sir."

I, also, had seen it. The movement of an arm. The constable ran to the stricken men, slipping on the blood but regaining his balance. "This one is alive."

We hurriedly approached at once, I wishing that I had brought my medical bag, but barely in time to hear a painful and almost inaudible exclamation before the man expired.

"Are you able to attend to this, constable?" Holmes asked. "Or shall we remain?"

The officer shook his head. "I would appreciate it, sir, if you would use your whistle again further along the street, for my sergeant will be passing in a few minutes. Can I tell him that you will be attending Scotland Yard, to report upon this?"

"Indeed. Kindly request also that he inform Inspector Gregson that we will be calling upon him."

Holmes enquired after the constable's name and assured him that it would be mentioned favourably, whereupon the officer thanked Holmes and saluted smartly as we left him.

"Did you hear what the dying man said, Holmes?" I asked as we emerged from the alley. "I could make nothing of it."

He blew the whistle loudly, as he had promised.

"It was indistinct, but his words were, 'You will regret the 27th'."

"That is not how it sounded."

"Of course not. He spoke in German."

I turned to him, surprised. "Then, after all, this is the work of Colonel Tomkins!"

"Or, more likely, one of his associates. The colonel, I think, is a little more sophisticated."

"As you have implied before. But what is the significance of the 27th?"

"The newspapers have revealed nothing as yet, but something official is evidently planned. Mycroft would know, but he will have been ordered to divulge nothing until his superiors consider the time to be appropriate. His own people may have already warned him that some sort of threat is imminent."

"Today is the 24th," I said as we searched for a hansom. "Perhaps some indication will present itself in the few days to come."

We returned to our lodgings in time for luncheon. The incident in the alley had upset my nerves, necessitating the consumption of a glass of brandy, but Holmes seemed unperturbed. I cannot say that much transpired for the remainder of the day, other than Holmes despatching several telegrams and, as the time for dinner neared, calling in his army of street Arabs, the Baker Street Irregulars. He gave them instructions to scour London for any indication of preparation for a forthcoming event, of any nature whatsoever. Anything that could be construed as intended for the 27th.

Dinner was, as I had expected, a solemn affair.

Holmes sat silently moving his food around his plate with a fork, eating nothing. The prospect of the 27th approaching, carrying with it some terrible threat about which he could do nothing was abhorrent to him, and had caused him to sink into the blackest of moods.

I recall that he spoke but once during our meal, breaking the silence briefly before sinking back into himself once more.

"But, Watson, this should not confound me. I should be able to define their intentions."

I made to reply, but saw at once that it would be hopeless to do so. Lost as deeply in his own thoughts as he was, I considered it doubtful that my friend would have heard me.

We heard Mrs Hudson upon the stairs and he rose and crossed the room to his usual armchair, moving stiffly in a machine-like manner. As she cleared away our plates, he gave no sign that he was aware of her presence. The lady looked at me questioningly, and I shook my head in response. Through the evening Holmes sat staring silently at the ceiling, no doubt considering and rejecting many courses of action. His eyes, like his entire expression, were blank, and after a while this caused me to feel uncomfortable. Each time I looked up from my reading it was to see that he had not moved but remained as he was, statue-like as the hours passed.

Finally I could endure this no more, and I resolved to retire early. I wished Holmes goodnight and experienced no surprise when he did not answer. I went to my bed with a troubled mind and a heavy heart.

Chapter 10 – A Deadly Distraction

As I sat down to breakfast, I saw that Holmes had already gone out. His food, untouched save for half the contents of the coffee pot, was removed by Mrs Hudson as she brought mine. In reply to my enquiry, she answered with concern that she had seen my friend briefly but that he had spoken hardly a word.

I knew from long experience the habits of Holmes. That he would remain absent until the evening I was certain, since this had been his invariable practice in all similar situations that I could bring to mind. It was then that it occurred to me that I had left my practice without attention for far too long. Dr Mickleborough was new to the profession, and therefore a locum that I had not used previously. I had instructed him to communicate with me by telegraph or messenger, should he encounter difficulty or any situation about which he felt unsure, but I had received no word. On the face of it then, all was well, but I am a man who seeks certainties in such things for his own peace of mind. I resolved to see at first hand whether the good doctor's capabilities had been equal to the often trying and exasperating complaints of some of my regular patients although, I admitted to myself, I had no reason to suppose otherwise.

As it was a fine day, I decided that a pleasant walk in St James or Hyde Park would be beneficial later, after which it would be late afternoon. I would then return to Baker Street for dinner and to await Holmes' reappearance.

The time passed without incident. Dr Mickleborough was quite pleased to see me, but I soon realised that my visit was unnecessary. After reassuring him that, though he did not appear to need my help, I was at his disposal as before, I enjoyed a luncheon of boiled ham at a coffee-shop as I made my way to St James, where I walked among tended lawns and along paths edged with trees and flowers. This lightened my spirits, although the prospect of my later meeting with Holmes now hung over me like a black cloud. After returning to our sitting room later, I perused a report about a measles epidemic in Northern England before eating a solitary dinner.

I had settled myself around the fireplace and filled my pipe, when I heard the door slam. Holmes bounded lightly up the stairs, causing me to hope that his day had gone well and that his mood had improved. His expression as he entered the room however, was disappointing.

"Ah, Watson! I trust that your day has been more fruitful than my own."

"You have made no progress, then?"

He hung up his hat and coat. "Very little, I regret to say. I sought out the Irregulars, who informed me that two funerals of people of some prominence will take place on the 27th. Also, I have recalled that a rather unpleasant fellow who I helped Lestrade put into Newgate will be released on that date. I went on to consult some of my other informers, with no result. Finally, I went to the Fleet Street offices of *The London Daily,* and afterwards to the Cheshire Cheese Tavern for a bite to eat and to hopefully glean something, but at no time did I discover the slightest reference to anything of significance."

"Then our only course is to watch and wait for something to indicate the whereabouts of Colonel Tomkins or the nature of whatever is to happen in two days' time."

"Precisely. But, as you are well aware, Watson, waiting does not lie well with me."

"Nevertheless, we have to be realistic. We must remain alert, so that no item of news or of hearsay escapes our attention." I smiled hesitantly, "At least you appear to be in better spirits, Holmes."

"For what good that does. Pah!" He crossed the room and threw himself into his usual armchair. I was about to ask him if I should call Mrs Hudson to bring him some food, when the door-bell rang loudly.

We fell silent and looked at each other.

"Are you expecting someone?" I asked.

He shook his head.

"Then perhaps this will be a new client, calling on the chance of an interview. A distraction will benefit you, I think."

"I have not the heart for it, but perhaps I can assist the lady."

I did not ask how he had concluded that our visitor was female, for I had seen him discern this and more from past clients' footfalls, many times.

The sounds from the stairs ceased and the door opened. Our landlady announced our visitor, a tall lady with shining red hair, as Mrs Hannah Beaumont, and paused as Holmes called for tea.

He had got to his feet already and, I have no doubt, deduced much from our client's strong and attractive features and dark green costume. After introducing us with a sudden, assumed pleasantness, he guided her to the basket chair and we seated ourselves.

"Your expression reveals that you have much to tell us, but pray delay your narrative until our landlady brings our tea. It will be no more than a few moments."

"Thank you, Mr Holmes," she replied in a rather husky voice. "You are most kind."

I rose at Mrs Hudson's knock, and took the tray from her at the door. After pouring and handing out cups, I resumed my seat and prepared myself to listen. Holmes drank, apparently in no hurry.

"Now that we have refreshed ourselves," he began when our cups were replaced, "please tell us how we can assist you. We are at your disposal."

"Thank you, gentlemen." She glanced at us both in turn. "The event I have to relate to you is curious, to say the least. Certainly, I can make nothing of it."

"We will do what we can to throw some light upon the situation. Pray take a moment to collect your thoughts, before beginning. Try not to omit the smallest detail."

Mrs Beaumont nodded. "I will try to relate what occurred exactly as I remember."

A heavily-laden cart rumbled along Baker Street as Holmes and I waited.

"Being newly arrived from Liverpool," she began. "My husband and I had decided to purchase a house in Holborn, a rather elderly place but with, we felt, much character. When we arrived there by appointment at three o'clock this afternoon, the front door was open and we entered, thinking that the agent of the concern selling it on behalf of the owner was awaiting us within. We peered into the spacious drawing-room, the parlour and the kitchen, to find them all deserted. Several times we called out, and my husband concluded that the agent must be deaf since there was no response. After a short while we climbed the stairs, by now considering it unlikely that we would be met but determined to see the upper floors before we made our decision. There we again found no one, and my husband suggested that I view the secondary room while he examined the master bedroom. This we did, and after a few minutes I went to join him. To my amazement the room was empty! My first thought was that he had moved to one of the other bedrooms, or even descended the stairs, so I proceeded to enter every room in the house calling his name. It soon became apparent that I was alone, and I could not imagine why he had quietly left the house without informing me. I took a cab back to the Grand Hotel, near Charing Cross Station, where we are staying, but I have not heard from him."

Holmes leaned back in his chair, staring at the ceiling, before he spoke. "Tell me, Mrs Beaumont, has your husband ever acted in this way before now? Is he given to sudden rash acts such as appearing suddenly at home, when you would expect him to be at his place of employment?"

She looked surprised at my friend's question. "Oh no, sir! George and I are very close. He would never do anything to cause me worry or anxiety. This is so unlike him. I considered enlisting the help of Scotland Yard, but as I said the facts are queer and I feared that I would be ridiculed or treated with amusement."

"Let us leave out the official force, for the moment. Describe to me the master bedroom, where your husband was last seen. Firstly, I take it that you actually *saw* him enter?"

"I did, Mr Holmes. We stood on the landing together, and I saw George walk through the doorway before I went to inspect the other room."

"After which you entered the master bedroom also?"

"It was no more than a minute or two later."

"Kindly give me your impressions of the room. For example, was there no window that he could have left by?"

"There was a single, very large window opposite the door, yes, but we were on the first floor and well above the ground. Also, it looked to me to be screwed down, as if it were never intended to be opened."

"Yes of course, the height." Holmes smiled briefly. "The walls, then. How were they decorated or painted?"

"The entire room was panelled in dark wood. I remember thinking that I would like to make some changes if we were to buy the house."

"In which direction does the house face, do you recall?"

After a moment, she nodded. "The agent mentioned that the front faces due west."

"And is the master bedroom at the front, or the rear?"

"The rear, I imagine so that the occupant's sleep will not be disturbed by noise from the street."

"Quite so." Holmes turned to me suddenly. "Watson, what thoughts have you on this?"

I considered quickly, taken unaware by this sudden attention. "All I can think of is that the panelling might have concealed a hidden door. Perhaps Mr Beaumont accidentally caused it to open, before being lured in by his own curiosity. If the door closed behind him, he would have been trapped."

"Quite so, old friend," he agreed. "But would he not then have hammered on the panels from the other side, surely to be heard by Mrs Beaumont?"

"That is most likely, unless he suffered a seizure or fainted."

Holmes turned to our client. "As far as you are aware, Mrs Beaumont, was your husband afflicted in this way?"

"Not at all. George is a strong man. I have never heard him mention that he has such a weakness."

"May I enquire as to his profession?"

"He is an accounts manager. Until we decided to move to the capital, he worked at the firm of Stokely & McKnight, who manufacture saddles and bridles. They were kind enough to transfer him to the London branch, at his request."

"Most convenient." Holmes rose suddenly as did I, followed by Mrs Beaumont. "It is certainly a puzzling tale you have told us, madam. I am inclined to think that your husband may return to you, even this late in the day. However, Watson and I will meet you at the house at, say, ten o'clock tomorrow morning, if that is convenient to you. If this mystery persists, we will attempt to clarify things then. Pray write down the address, and I am certain that soon all will be well."

She complied at once and thanked us profusely before leaving. I accompanied her to the front door and hailed a cab, before returning to our sitting-room to find Holmes watching from the window.

"You found a hansom for her," he observed. "I should not have been surprised if her employers, confederates or whatever they are, had been waiting in a hired coach."

"What can you mean, Holmes?" I retorted.

He laughed mirthlessly. "Come, Watson. Have you not realised that her entire story is a fiction, doubtlessly designed to induce us to enter the house in Holborn? I really must commend Colonel Tomkins for his persistence."

'When did you reach such a conclusion?"

"The instant I heard the lady speak."

"Her voice was perhaps somewhat deep for a woman, but I do not see…"

"Do you recall the woman we observed leaving the warehouse in Lambeth? She was there, of course, to call out to us from the darkness within, creating the impression that she had taken refuge from those pursuing her. The two men accompanying her were doubtless ready to fire upon us."

"A tall woman," I remembered, "with black hair."

Holmes nodded. "And a voice that carried sufficiently for me to recognise traces of a Hamburg accent, which she has evidently gone to some trouble to eradicate."

"You believe that Mrs Beaumont is that woman?"

"No, I *know* that they are one and the same. Oh, do not allow the red hair to deceive you, I saw traces of dye on the back of her neck during the interview. Also, it struck me at once how little concerned she appeared, after making it clear to us that she and her husband enjoyed close intimacy."

"So this, again, is a trap?"

"Most certainly. I had intended to despatch telegrams to both the Liverpool and London branches of Stokely & McKnight, to verify our visitor's claim regarding her husband's employment, but I quickly realised that the effort is unnecessary. In the morning we will pause on our way to Holborn, long enough to inform Scotland Yard of our discoveries and intentions."

"Inspector Gregson, having dismissed Mr Josiah Endicott's fears so lightly, is likely to be surprised."

"It is certain that he will be. However, I hope he has the good sense to attend us at the house."

"You intend that we should go there, then?"

"Certainly."

Holmes hurried through a scant breakfast the following morning, then took to pacing the room impatiently as he waited for me to finish my toast.

"We will send the telegram to Gregson from the first Post Office we pass," he reminded me as we put on our hats and coats. This was soon accomplished, and we arrived a short while later in a short tree-lined street called Cedar Avenue to find Mrs Beaumont outside the house, awaiting us on the steps.

She greeted us brightly as the hansom left. Although she maintained a calm appearance I saw uncertainty, apprehension perhaps, in her eyes.

Holmes scrutinised the exterior of the house, before requesting that we be accompanied to the master bedroom.

"Is the room normally kept locked?" he asked Mrs Beaumont as we ascended the stairs together.

"I would think that the previous owner secured the door, probably at night. The key is still within the room in the lock."

My friend nodded, smiling faintly.

The landing was wide and the door of the master bedroom, which Mrs Beaumont indicated, stood slightly ajar. Holmes pushed it open slowly, appearing to examine the floor within. Suddenly, with a speed that startled me, he withdrew the key and stepped back. He then slammed the door shut and locked it, before dropping the key in his pocket.

Mrs Beaumont's manner changed instantly. "Mr Holmes, what are you doing? I do not understand."

He looked at her severely. "I am certain that you do, Madam. The patch of light from the window shining upon the floor confirms my suspicions instantly. I fear that you and your friends will not be returning to Germany for a good while, possibly never."

Her expression hardened then, her mouth becoming a straight line and her eyes set in a cruel glare. "One day, when we are the masters of all of Europe, we will destroy you and your interfering kind, Mr Holmes. You cannot resist us forever."

"That remains to be seen, I think. In any event, it will not be today. However, you will have the opportunity to elaborate further on your intentions, very shortly."

With that he produced his police whistle and blew it loudly. The echoes had hardly died away before we heard heavy footfalls upon the stairs, and Inspector Gregson appeared with five constables.

"Ah, Gregson," said my friend. "Allow me to introduce Mrs Beaumont. That is not her real name of course, since she is a German agent visiting our country for hostile purposes." He retrieved the key and handed it to the official detective. "In the room before you are several of her accomplices who are surely armed, so it is as well that your men are also. After their arrest I am quite certain that much will be learned from them before long, and should the name 'Colonel Tomkins' be mentioned, I would be obliged if you would inform me."

At this, the woman spat out a succession of oaths in German. Holmes, completely unmoved, wished everyone a pleasant morning after assuring the inspector that he would submit a report to Scotland Yard in the near future. As we descended the stairs I heard Gregson issuing harsh orders.

There were no cabs to be seen in Cedar Avenue, so we walked in the direction of the High Street at a fast pace.

"Holmes, how did you know what awaited you in that room?" I enquired as we reached the end of the street.

"It was not a difficult conclusion. You will recall that I had already deduced that our client was a German agent, so our reception here was certain to be hostile. Thus, it remained only to define the nature of the threat. When 'Mrs Beaumont' requested my help, she mentioned that the master bedroom had a window that was situated opposite the door. Since she was good enough to answer my question about the direction towards which the house faces, west as it happened, we know that the rear of the premises, where the master bedroom is, faces east."

"Where the sun rises," I ventured.

"Precisely. I knew therefore that the shadow of anyone concealed behind the door within the room would cast a shadow upon the floor, which is what I saw. There were, in fact, several waiting in various positions that I could make out in the brief instant before I locked them in."

"Clearly, they wished to be certain of your demise."

"Indeed. The Germans have a reputation for thoroughness," he said as he summoned a hansom.

Chapter 11 – Die Kanonen

After our experiences of the morning, Mrs Hudson's steak pie was a most welcome luncheon.

"Do you expect to hear from Gregson soon, Holmes?" I enquired as we finished our coffee.

We rose from the table and made our way to our armchairs around the fireplace. "I am not certain that we will do so at all. Scotland Yard do not generously share information normally, and I confess that I am relying on our past assistance to them to cause the inspector to feel justified in confiding in us."

"We wait, then?"

"Only until I can make some further enquiries. I will now smoke a pipe with you, old friend, before I set out. No, do not look expectantly at the coat-rack, for I will not require to be accompanied."

Surprised and with my feelings slightly hurt at this, I put a light to my pipe and threw the vesta into the empty grate. As it turned out Holmes never left, for the door-bell rang loudly as he replaced his pipe in the rack. We listened in silence as our landlady spoke to the caller who was apparently known to her, since she allowed him to ascend the stairs unaccompanied.

"Gregson," said Holmes, reverting to a normal sitting position from a listening posture. "I did not expect a visit."

The inspector knocked at our door and my friend bade him enter. When greetings had been exchanged and our visitor had seated himself, Holmes looked at him curiously.

"By your expression and your presence here, I perceive that something is amiss. What is it, Gregson?"

The official detective had a look of anger and disappointment about him, and a few moments passed before he answered.

"It was taken out of our hands, Mr Holmes."

"The affair of this morning?"

Inspector Gregson nodded. "No sooner had we begun to question the prisoners than a party of men arrived at the Yard. The Assistant Commissioner accompanied them and insisted that we release the German agents into their custody. It was a slap in the face for us, I can tell you, but we had no choice but to obey."

"I can sympathise with your feelings, Inspector, but were you given any indication as to the identities of these newcomers?"

"Only that they were all superior to us in rank."

"Did the prisoners appear relieved, to be handed over to them?"

"Not at all, sir. If anything, they appeared more fearful."

Holmes' expression deepened. "Did any of them say anything of significance, either previously or as they were led away?"

"It was mostly a jumble of utterances in their own language. I heard the end of something the woman said to one of the others. It sounded like 'Die kanonen', as near as I could make out. One of her comrades was at pains to quieten her quickly."

"Most interesting." Holmes smiled faintly. "However, I would not concern yourself over their fate. They have been taken from you to face more intensive questioning, I am sure. The government have people who are experts in extracting information from those who mean harm to our country."

"I am sure that is so, and I wish them success regardless." Gregson rose to his feet. "Well, gentlemen, that is what I came to tell you. I am afraid you can expect no further assistance from Scotland Yard regarding this affair, though I confess that I would like to know the outcome. For now I have other enquiries to pursue, so I will bid you good-day."

"Our thanks to you, Gregson. It seems that little remains to be done."

We shook hands and the inspector left. When we were again seated, I turned to my friend: "Your brother's doing, I presume?"

"There is certainly Mycroft's hand in this. His people must have been following this enquiry closely, to have acted so swiftly. I would not care to share the fate of any of the prisoners."

"What of the remark made by 'Mrs Beaumont'?"

Holmes considered thoughtfully. "That, I think, reveals to us the nature of the activity at Mendells Lodge."

I paused before answering, listening to the cries of a newspaper-seller in Baker Street. The early editions were evidently available.

"I cannot see how."

"Her words were 'Die Kanonen', Watson. *The Cannon.* Can you not see the significance?"

"They were constructing a weapon, a cannon, at Mendells Lodge?"

"Precisely. It must be a gun of exceptional range and power, for them to have needed to manufacture it in this way."

"But for what purpose?"

"That is what we must find out. We must scour the newspapers for an announcement of a forthcoming event which will certainly have national importance. I cannot imagine that our German friends would go to such lengths for anything less."

Holmes sent many telegrams that day. Despite our efforts nothing was revealed to us, and as the day wore on I felt increased anxieties. Because of our long association I had become familiar with my friend's ways, and so I experienced no surprise that he appeared calm, unconcerned even. Sleep eluded me for most of that night, and Holmes paced relentlessly in his room.

The 27th dawned and the remaining replies to Holmes' telegrams arrived. In every case he screwed them up and cast them aside in disgust. I began an examination of the morning papers as he prowled around the room, beset by melancholia and ill-temper. At length he seized his hat and coat and announced:

"There is nothing else for it. I am going to see Mycroft. Kindly inform Mrs Hudson that I may not be in for luncheon. I require no company, Watson, on this occasion."

With that he left abruptly. Again feeling rather put out, I resumed my inspection of the dailies. This proved unfruitful, and I had long since put them aside when he returned.

"Mycroft was in a jovial mood, but no help at all," he informed me. "Likewise, Scotland Yard. All that I learned there was that Lestrade is back from Aberdeen, and that he is not pleased with the amount of work that has accumulated on his desk during his absence."

"I regret that I have discovered nothing in the papers, Holmes."

He took off his hat and coat and stood completely still. To my astonishment, his grim expression changed in an instant. He actually smiled after consulting his pocket-watch.

"I see that the hour for dinner is almost upon us. While scouring the streets of London I made certain arrangements, so that I will be notified by telegraph should events such as we have been anticipating occur during the remainder of the day. I must say that Colonel Tomkins is leaving it rather late, if he intends to act as we expected."

We had almost finished our meal, the coffee pot emptied and the plates cleared away, before I saw my opportunity to ask:

"Holmes, you look positively relieved. Your mood has changed. What have you discovered?"

He pushed away his empty cup and took on a nonchalant air. "I am now doubtful that we shall receive any news during the few hours that remain of this day but, as I have mentioned, precautions for our notification are in hand."

"Then the 27th was incorrect? It was uttered to misguide us, perhaps?"

"That is possible, but I think it unlikely that a man would do that as his life slipped away. No, Watson, I believe he spoke the truth. We naturally understood that he meant the 27th of the present month, but that seems not to be the case. If we monitor carefully the events of the next few weeks, something may present itself before the 27th of *next* month."

We did indeed maintain our watch in all directions open to us, for any indication of a situation that could be exploited by our adversaries. When nothing proved to be forthcoming, Holmes turned his attention to other matters brought to him by the daily post. I have recounted elsewhere, 'The Incident of Markova's Mask' and 'The Adventure of the Terrified Teacher'. Holmes dismissed these, as he sometimes did, as 'trifling' and therefore unworthy of the attention of my readers, but I maintain the hope that he will one day relent and permission will be given for me to disclose all.

Shortly before these cases were concluded, the notes began. At first they were warnings of unspecified troubles to come and Holmes, who had received many such communications over the years, paid them little heed following his usual examination. But when references to our dear Queen began to appear, and then a mention of the 27th, my friend at once gave them renewed attention. He had, in any case, reverted to considering the unsolved case involving Colonel Tomkins, since all his other outstanding investigations were now resolved.

The seventh note was delivered by post on the morning of the 21st.

"Up until now, Watson, I have been able to make nothing of any of these warnings. I presume that the writer wore gloves at the times of their composition, for there was not so much as a smudge on the paper. Always they were written in capital letters, in green ink and, I suspect from the constant slight spattering effect, with the same pen."

"This time then, is different?" I said, lowering myself into my armchair after breakfast.

"That is likely. There is a hair trapped in the envelope which may tell me something, but we shall see."

With that he crossed the room to where the table containing his chemical experiments stood. After a moment he tipped the contents of the envelope onto a glass slide which he placed under his microscope, and a short silence followed as he studied it closely.

"It is indeed hair," he concluded at last, "which doubtlessly once adorned a human head, but it has been coated with something." He paused, resuming after a moment. "Ah, I have it!"

"You can learn something of the sender, from that?"

He looked up. "Not unless he or she is a dummy, or a doll. This hair has been treated with a preparation such as is used in the making of a wig for the purpose of decorating an effigy."

"A visit to one of your theatrical acquaintances may be revealing, then. A ventriloquist?", I ventured.

"My first thought was similar, but something about this troubles me. There was an article that I recently pasted into my index, I think."

With that he rose abruptly and seized the current volume from the shelf. On his hands and knees, he began to turn the pages frantically while I looked on.

"Aha!" he cried at length, suddenly still as he read to himself the contents of the discovered article. "I believe we have something here, Watson."

A few minutes passed before he closed and replaced the volume. He resumed his seat around the fireplace with an air of triumph.

"What is it, Holmes?"

He leaned forward, as if he wished to be sure that I heard clearly. "There have been several recent reports in the daily press regarding the sudden disappearance of Mr Harold Cranmore MP. The official explanation is that he is currently on a diplomatic mission to Paris, but I have the gravest doubts as to the truth of that as such a task would not normally fall within his scope. However, it is the mention of his wife's activities that interests me. I have read of them before now."

"You believe that she is somehow involved?"

"I believe that it is possible that it is she who is the author of the succession of letters that we have received. If that is so, then the information they contain would have been obtained from her husband, probably without his knowledge, and can therefore be considered reliable. Such being the case, we must concentrate once more on the hidden activities of Colonel Tomkins and his friends, since the letters mention the 27th."

I sat up straight, suddenly alarmed. "Our Queen was mentioned also, and you previously spoke of a cannon. Are these German agents intending an assassination?"

"Excellent, Watson. That is my conclusion also. Let us retrieve our hats and coats and visit Camberwell, where we may learn more of this."

"But what can we expect to discover there, and why do you believe that Mrs Cranmore sent the letters?"

"A perusal of the article in my index suggests her as the most likely author." He moved restlessly in his chair, impatient to follow this new scent. "Consider, she runs a shop in Camberwell, for the benefit of charity. There she sells goods that have been regularly donated by various individuals, and most of those mentioned have one thing in common: they are all makers or former makers of dolls and puppets."

We procured a hansom quickly, as a fare was delivered near our lodgings almost at the moment we set out. Holmes said little on the way to Camberwell, but directed the driver to bring his horse to a halt near Orpheus Street, where a long row of shops were situated opposite a laundry.

"Further down, past the undertaker's parlour, I think," my friend said to me as the cab left us.

We strode through the crowd of window-gazers, servants engaged upon their master's shopping and nannies with their charges until we came upon a narrow little shop with its door open. Stepping inside, we found ourselves in semi-darkness and surrounded by dolls of many likenesses and sizes. For some reason I found their empty stares uncomfortable, but Holmes was unaffected. He allowed his eyes to take in the vacant expressions and gaudy apparel, before approaching the counter and ringing the bell.

A woman immediately emerged from behind a curtain, revealing for an instant an inner chamber. Both her hair and general appearance told me that she was a lady of quality and, although well past her youth, of some attraction. Her voice, as she greeted us, confirmed her status, but her eyes were at once wary and sad.

"Good morning, Mrs Cranmore," replied Holmes. "I see from your expression that you recognise me and are probably aware of why we are here. Let me assure you that I have made myself familiar with your situation and will assist you in any way that I can." He gestured in my direction. "This is my friend and associate of whom you may have heard, Doctor John Watson. Please believe me when I tell you that you are as safe in speaking before him as you are to me."

The lady acknowledged me. "Thank you, gentlemen. My anxiety has been increasing for weeks, as I have been so concerned. I did not know where to turn, since I am disobeying my husband with my actions. I wrote to you anonymously in the hope that you would define the truth of the facts I have discovered. I did not dare to identify myself." She paused, adopting a puzzled expression. "But how did you come to realise that it was I who sent the warnings, Mr Holmes?"

"It is my business to see into such things, Madam."

"Yes, of course." She moved towards the door and closed it, displaying the sign proclaiming that the shop was currently not open for business. "Now we will not be disturbed, and I will tell you all."

She proceeded to relate a tale of her husband's curious behaviour. He had been uncharacteristically withdrawn for some time so that she had begun to suspect that he was ill, which he curtly denied. He spoke to her less and less until they were like strangers, and she concluded that the source of his unhappiness was his work. It was then that Mrs Cranmore made a rash decision. She resolved to settle this matter, or at least to understand it. One day, when she knew he was fulfilling his duties in parliament, she unlocked her husband's desk using the spare key from a hiding-place which she had discovered accidentally, long before.

Among his papers were documents that were clearly of a sensitive nature, and should never have been removed from Whitehall. Also, there was a signed confession of all her husband's actions, to be opened in the event of his death. She had seen, as Holmes had, the intended conclusion of it all, yet she could not inform the official force without revealing herself. Hence the hints in the letters to Baker Street and our eventual presence here today.

At the end of her narrative, he regarded her grimly.

"You must realise, Madam, that there is only one penalty for treason."

Tearfully, she wrung her hands. "But Mr Holmes, I have not yet explained the reason behind these acts."

"Then pray do so."

"It was because of our daughter, Julia. Harold would never have considered doing what he has done, otherwise."

"She has been threatened?" I enquired.

"Worse than that, she has been abducted. We received a telegram from the school she attends, Our Lady of Divine Grace, in Norfolk, informing us that she had suddenly ceased to be present at classes. Enquiries at her accommodation revealed that the premises were empty, and had been so for several days."

"When was this discovered?" asked Holmes.

"It must be several weeks ago, now. I am sorry, gentlemen, I am so confused."

"How did you become sure of her abduction?"

The conversation was momentarily interrupted by someone attempting to enter the shop. Several times the door-knob was rattled vigorously. We were standing where we could not be seen, and said no more until the caller left and silence returned.

Mrs Cranmore was clearly fighting back tears, but she bravely continued. "The day after we discovered Julia's disappearance found both my husband and I becoming mad with uncertainty and grief. Sometime later a man called at our Mayfair home and asked to see us. I knew from the moment I set eyes upon him that my daughter's fate was in his hands, because of the way he had concealed his features. Despite the warm weather, he had wrapped a thick muffler around his face and turned the collar of his coat up. He also wore a wide-brimmed hat, which he had pulled well down. He informed us, in a very calm voice, that Julia was safe and well, and would remain so as long as my husband supplied certain information which had previously been asked of him. His unusual behaviour of before was now explained: he had not responded to previous threats, but ignored them. This, now, was to ensure his obedience. You can see, gentlemen, the dilemma in which we were placed."

Holmes nodded. "Did Mr Cranmore divulge to you the information that was demanded?"

"Not at all. That is why I sought the nature of their demands in his desk. I could not bear the thought, nor the disgrace, of what I suspected him to be engaged upon. Even with Julia at stake, I had to act somehow." She clasped her hands strongly together, hopelessness written on her face. "I beg of you, Mr Holmes, try to save my daughter and my husband."

"You have my word that I will do what I can. The position that your husband and yourself found yourselves in is very clear to me and I perceive the reason for your actions. Others may see the situation differently, but I will see what can be done. I can promise nothing, however."

Nevertheless, her face showed some relief. "Thank you, sir. You have at least given me a grain of hope."

"Madam," Holmes said as some calm returned to her, "if we are to help you, there is something we must know."

"Something from my husband's papers?"

"Indeed. If you have learned from them the significance of the 27th pray tell us, for I suspect this to be a key to the furtherance of our investigation."

She hesitated, I thought because the answer was not yet common knowledge. Then: "Very well. My husband's notes refer to a parade that is to take place in the capital on that date. Her Majesty is to attend."

Chapter 12 – The Rescue

At least another hour must have passed, before Holmes and I left Mrs Cranmore. The lady now appeared to be in better spirits than when we arrived, probably because she had derived some little hope from Holmes' promise. He had questioned her closely, until he was certain that she knew nothing more that could aid our investigation. Always he adopted his most reasonable and sympathetic *persona* to avoid further disturbing her obviously fragile nervous state, and I reflected that this was an occasion where Holmes, the cold reasoner, allowed his human traits to reveal themselves.

We procured a passing hansom with ease, and Holmes was about to shout to the driver the address of our Baker Street lodgings when he became suddenly very still. Leaning forward in his seat, he peered into the street as if to observe something of interest but I could see nothing except two mature ladies, holding their bonnets in place because of the wind that had sprung up. A rather tall fellow desperately raised his arm, and a cab from the opposite direction slowed and came to a halt near him. He boarded and evidently instructed the driver to progress with all speed, since the horse immediately took off at a fast trot.

"Driver," Holmes resumed, "Be so good as to follow that cab. An extra half-sovereign if you do not lose it and deliver us to the same destination undetected."

Our cabbie was clearly no stranger to such a situation. As we passed through the streets of Camberwell he slowed his horse, keeping the other hansom barely in sight but never encroaching upon the distance he had apparently set.

We eventually found ourselves on the left bank of the Thames, following through Limehouse and Blackwall. Holmes, who had spoken only occasionally during the journey, murmured something that I only just caught.

"We are approaching the West India Docks. I do not believe that our pursuit has been noticed. Our cabbie has done well."

"Why are we following this man?"

"Did you not notice him watching Mrs Cranmore's shop? He was there as we entered and as we left. As we emerged he was careful to make himself scarce, before hailing the cab. He is, I think, about to report our visit there to his superiors. I have great hopes that Colonel Tomkins will be among them."

Ahead, the tall man alighted and made off quickly. Holmes called to our driver who brought the horse to a halt. I handed the man some coins and he saluted before turning the hansom around and leaving. We were now alone in a deserted side-street, made the more gloomy by the cloud that had obscured the sun. Before us were warehouses and square buildings that I assumed contained shipping offices or lodging houses for sailors in transit. Holmes strode, with me in his wake, past a dismal structure displaying a faded notice that identified it as a Seaman's Mission.

"Wait, Watson!" He placed a restraining arm on my shoulder as the tall man turned a corner. "That was the moment when he was most likely to look back."

We waited until enough time had passed, by Holmes' estimation, for our quarry to have approached his destination. Through a gap in the buildings ahead I could see a narrow view of the Thames, with tugs and other small boats passing constantly back and forth. We could hear much activity from the nearby dock area and I caught a glimpse of a tall crane, swinging its bundled load away from the vessel that had brought it.

Holmes peered quickly around the corner, and then drew back.

"There is a group of large terraced houses forming one side of the street. The man we are following has gained entry to the first of these, after volunteering some sort of password."

"How can we follow further?"

"We cannot, and yet I am reluctant to call out the official force without knowing what is happening in there." He pointed across the street. "If we can gain entry to the rear of the property by the use of that gate, we may be able to make certain that our friend's accomplices are there also."

After a few moments we approached the gate, walking normally so as not to arouse the suspicions of the few people who had appeared along the street. We received no attention as we lifted the latch and entered, after he had knocked back the single bolt with his walking-cane. Holmes closed he gate silently and we ignored the path leading to the other houses, stepping over the low fence and approaching a heavily-curtained window. He put his ear to the glass and waited before smiling grimly, drawing me back and speaking in a low voice.

"They are there. I heard them speaking in German. Of Colonel Tomkins I am unsure, but I'll wager that the rest of his group, or most of them, are no more than a few feet away from us at this moment. On the way here I noticed a Post Office not more than half a mile away. I would be grateful, old fellow, if you would telegraph Gregson with the news. I think perhaps he may be interested now."

I was about to comply when the curtain was pulled back roughly. It was unlikely that we had been overheard, I thought, since the man who was revealed appeared totally surprised. He squinted at us, his mouth agape with astonishment, before crying out loudly. Then the rear door was flung open to reveal three others who glared at us furiously. One of them reached into his coat and produced a pistol as the others drew back to give him a clear field of fire.

"Run, Watson." Holmes pushed me away from the house, and in a moment we were through the gate and back in the street. I had heard one report as we attained the path, but the bullet had gone wide.

When we had gained enough ground, we slowed breathlessly to a fast walk.

"Holmes, I think it would be best if I set off."

"You saw where the Post Office was situated?"

"I did. I will hurry, and procure a hansom if one presents itself, but what will you do?"

He peered quickly back, to ensure that we were not pursued. "I shall return to the vicinity of that house and conceal myself. If they leave, I will endeavour to follow."

I saw no cab but strode quickly until I was able to get assistance from a fellow driving a milk cart. He was good enough to take me to within sight of my destination and I was grateful, despite my fear that the rattling churns behind us would overturn. I gave him some coins and alighted. Minutes later I scribbled out a message and handed the telegram to the rather befuddled Postmaster, stressing its urgency. I had informed Gregson as to our whereabouts in detail, and I now realised that the police coach would pass the Post Office on its way to join Holmes, since there was no other route. I was therefore presented with the dilemma of either remaining outside to be picked up as the vehicle passed, or hurrying back to join my friend. As I could not ascertain how long it would take for Scotland Yard to act, I retraced my steps with all the speed I could muster, determined to render Holmes any assistance that I could.

At last I found myself within sight of the house. My efforts had again left me rather breathless, and I had constantly watched for pursuers or any kind of threat. The street was as deserted as before, and I could see no sign of activity within the house or of Holmes.

Then the front door opened slightly, and I retreated into concealment. A man who I recognised as he who had fired upon us peered out. He glanced cautiously up and down the street before, apparently satisfied that the coast was clear, gesturing to those within. Three more men, all brandishing pistols, emerged and began an examination of doorways and all possible hiding-places nearby. I saw that they were seeking to ensure that they were not under observation, possibly as a prelude to their departure, after being alerted by our visit. I began to fear that they might discover Holmes or myself, at any moment.

Further along the street a single beech had grown and spread its branches wide. One of the armed searchers stood beneath it, staring intently into the thick mass of leaves. As he turned away I heard frantic movement within the branches, causing him to return his attention at once and to discharge his weapon. The echo rebounded from the buildings and leaves

146

floated slowly to the pavement as a pigeon, terrified after its narrow escape, flew into view before vanishing behind the houses. I let out a sigh of relief, thankful that the tree had not, as I had begun to suspect, concealed Holmes.

The next moment produced my own peril, for another German who I had been distracted from by watching the first had drawn near enough to detect my presence. He shouted something in an urgent tone, his native language sounding harsh to my ears, before firing twice. I dropped to the pavement and struggled to draw my service weapon as the bullets struck the door behind me. Before I could retaliate another report sounded loud and the man who had fired threw up his arms and fell. I had a brief impression of a face withdrawing from an upstairs window of a building opposite, before the remaining spies, having realised my location, began approaching.

Holmes, it seemed, had identified a vacant house and used it as an observation-post, probably after using his pick-lock. Once again I reflected that, despite the imminent danger, my friend had come to my aid and saved my life.

The man nearest to me raised his pistol. I struggled to my feet, firing as I did so. He may not have realised that I was armed, for an expression of absolute surprise crossed his face as he fell. More shots came from the window, and some of the others turned away to return fire. The window shattered, and I prayed that Holmes was unharmed. I took refuge around a corner as a bullet struck the brickwork near my face, and waited with my weapon ready. From this position I could see two more armed men emerging from the house, and it came to me that our situation was hopeless. I peered out and barely had time to retreat before a fusillade spilled dust and brick fragments into the air. Holmes fired again but was forced to take cover by rapid retaliation, and one man attempted to enter the building by the door below. I could not see them, but I sensed that those remaining were closing in. I realised that our adversaries might be greater in number than I knew, since more could easily have appeared from the house while my attention was concentrated on my defence. A loud crash caused me to glance across the street, where I saw that one of the men who had fired at Holmes was kicking frantically at the door while the other kept his pistol trained on the window above. I could not see that we could defeat so many, nor that we would survive, for in an instant I would face a barrage from several directions. But then a coach thundered into the street, and came to an abrupt halt. Gregson and four constables alighted, already firing at our assailants.

The horses, alarmed by the noise, reared up, but the driver immediately set them on at a fast trot out of harm's way. Near the opposite corner, one of the constables fell with gritted teeth as blood dripped from his left arm. Holmes appeared in the doorway of his refuge ready to continue firing, but Gregson and the other men had already cut down all opposition save for two who dropped their weapons in surrender.

Two constables quickly secured them in handcuffs and, with their injured comrade, marched them around the corner where the coach presumably waited. Holmes, Gregson and I searched the immediate area carefully, ensuring that none of the spies had concealed themselves in the doorways, as the remaining constable stood guard outside the house.

"Are you gentlemen injured?" The official detective enquired when we were satisfied.

Holmes and I looked at each other, shaking our heads.

"Your arrival was most timely," my friend acknowledged. "Thank you, Gregson."

"As luck would have it, I had just returned to the Yard when Doctor Watson's telegram arrived. These, I take it, are members of the spy ring about which we have been told so little?"

"Indeed." Holmes looked in the direction of the house. "But I have no means of knowing how many more may be inside. Also, I have reason to believe that there is a hostage."

Gregson followed his gaze. "Very well. We will find out." He turned to the constable. "Remain alert and keep your weapon to hand, Merrett. Accompany us."

The four of us entered cautiously. Two rooms led off the hallway, and it was obvious from their condition that the house had been unoccupied for some months. Ahead of us was a steep flight of uncarpeted stairs, narrow so that we were obliged to ascend in single file. Gregson, as the representative of the official force, hastened to be the first to begin the climb, with Holmes and myself after him and the constable bringing up the rear. The inspector had climbed about half-way, before he was able to see anything of the landing before him. He suddenly became very still.

"What is it, Gregson?" Holmes asked.

"Come up, all of you," a new voice said.

We all continued our ascent, to finally set foot upon the wide landing. A heavy, bearded man who was unknown to me stood near the entrance to the nearest room, holding a shotgun. He held the weapon not pointed in our direction, but inserted in a small and ragged hole in the door. This puzzled me but I saw that Holmes, and possibly Gregson, understood at once.

The Inspector raised his revolver. "Take care! If you fire we will cut you down at once. Your only chance is to give yourself up to us."

"Much to the contrary." The bearded man's voice held only a faint trace of his native German accent. "It is I who have the upper hand. Unless you gentlemen relinquish your firearms and let me depart, I will certainly discharge mine. Directly in line with my aim, our hostage sits bound hand and foot. He cannot escape death while in that position, and he cannot move away from it. His importance to you is known to us, but he has been of limited use to our purpose. That my life will also end at your hands is unimportant when considered in the light of the future of Imperial Germany. So I put it to you, gentlemen, will you choose to let him live, or die?"

"They were well prepared for a situation such as this," I observed quietly.

"Who is their hostage?" Gregson asked Holmes.

"Harold Cranmore, the Member of Parliament who recently disappeared."

The Inspector considered for a moment, then lowered his pistol with great reluctance. "Very well. We have no choice."

I believe that it had occurred to Holmes that the man would be powerless once he had withdrawn his weapon from the door, since then the situation would be reduced to four firearms against one, but our adversary was not so easily bested.

"So then, you gentlemen will oblige me by entering the room to your left and closing the door," he said seriously.

"Once inside, you will lock the door before pushing the key out under it. That will provide me with adequate time to make my exit."

"And what is to prevent you killing your hostage before leaving?" enquired Gregson.

"I beg that you allow that I am, like yourselves, a man of honour. It is not only Englishmen who are bound by their word. I regret, I can offer no other assurance."

We saw no alternative, andz complied. Before the door was fully closed behind us, Holmes was standing at the window at an angle that probably could not be seen from the street. I joined him but we saw nothing, and after a few minutes it became obvious that our enemy had escaped by the rear door and fled across the gardens to the Thames.

"I will watch from the other room as soon as I can," I volunteered. "It faces the back of the house."

"As you will, Watson, but I fear it is already too late."

At that, the constable delivered two hefty kicks to the door, splitting the lower panel immediately. He then reached through and retrieved the key, and in moments we stood on the landing among a litter of shattered wood.

I at once entered the opposite chamber. One glance across the gardens and the Thames confirmed that my friend was correct. The man was nowhere in sight.

Gregson, I knew, was furious at the way things had turned out, but he hid his anger admirably as he called to the prisoner.

"Mr Cranmore, can you hear me?" he cried, and we heard a muffled reply.

The constable and I put our shoulders to the door, and it gave to our third charge. We rushed in to find a man bound hand and foot to a heavy chair of stout oak, with a ball of rags stuffed into his mouth and held in place by bandages.

Holmes and Gregson released him carefully, and I immediately administered brandy from my flask. It was apparent from his inability to walk at first that he had been tied and restrained for a considerable time, affecting his circulation.

"They deceived me," he struggled to tell us presently. "I believed that I was working for our government, to ensure the safety of the parade. They were convincing, passing themselves off as our own people, and I was taken in."

"Did they harm you?" enquired Holmes as I completed my examination.

"I was deprived of food and drink, and suffered several blows. That was all, but I was told that my ordeal had not yet begun. We were awaiting a man I had met previously as Major Danvers of the Home Office, who I eventually realised was a German agent."

Holmes glanced at me and I knew he same question had entered both our minds: was Major Danvers actually Colonel Tomkins? Mr Cranmore's description of the major was inconclusive but, as Holmes remarked, to change his appearance would have posed him little difficulty.

Some of the colour had returned to Mr Cranmore's face, by the time Gregson called a halt to the proceedings.

"We will have a police coach here for you soon, sir. You will be taken to your wife and to consume some food, and your personal physician will be informed. You will also be guarded, for the time being. I hope that is satisfactory."

Mr Cranmore, still unsteady on his feet, affirmed this. I wondered how long it would be, before Mycroft Holmes intervened.

Inspector Gregson ordered the constable to join the waiting coach and return to the Yard with the prisoners, and then to despatch another conveyance to collect Mr Cranmore, Holmes and myself. We had some time to wait in the rather neglected drawing-room and, after some carefully-phrased questions to the politician by Gregson, Holmes made use of it.

"Mr Cranmore," he began, "I trust you are feeling somewhat recovered."

The politician smiled weakly. "Except for considerable hunger, yes. I cannot thank you gentlemen sufficiently for your actions in securing my release from these criminals. May I ask, how did you come to know where I was being held?"

"There were a number of indicators which, when considered together, pointed us in the right direction," Holmes answered. "I am still at a loss to understand one aspect of all this, however."

"I will enlighten you, if I can."

"Thank you, sir. It concerns your mention of a forthcoming parade. Had I known of this, we might have arrived here sooner." As he finished speaking, I saw Holmes glance at Gregson from the corner of his eye.

"I believe the news was to be released to the newspapers, later today," Mr Cranmore said, "so there is no reason now that I cannot divulge that there is to be a procession on the 27th, with Her Majesty in attendance."

Chapter 13 – The Parade

Holmes and I glanced at each other.

"What is it to commemorate?" he enquired.

"The official visit of the Maharajah of Tipoor, one of the lesser Indian native states. He has specifically requested a procession of the Royal Horse Artillery, which has been granted."

"I do not believe that Mr Holmes requires any further explanation, sir." Gregson said then. It did not surprise me that he resented civilians learning of this before the official force had been notified.

Mr Cranmore, I thought, looked slightly embarrassed, but before anyone could speak further the awaited police coach arrived. As we left the house I noticed Holmes glance in every direction, alert to the possibility that one of the spies could still be lying in wait since we were unaware of the exact number of the ring. Our journey was uneventful however, and a scowling Gregson was good enough to deposit us in Baker Street on his way to deliver Mr Cranmore to whatever fate awaited him, before returning to Scotland Yard.

"What will become of Mr Cranmore, now?" I asked Holmes as we ascended the stairs.

"There is no way to tell. Whatever his reason, his actions were a serious betrayal of trust, although we now know that he did not at first realise that he was dealing with the enemy. I will speak to Mycroft, but beyond that I am helpless to intervene."

We settled ourselves in our sitting-room, noting that it was now late afternoon. Mrs Hudson appeared almost at once with plates of cold meat and coffee, stating concernedly that we had missed luncheon and that this food was intended to fortify us until dinner. I ate hungrily while Holmes did so without enthusiasm, and it was shortly after we had cleared our plates that the door-bell rang. Moments later, our landlady announced "Mr Mycroft Holmes".

We both rose, my friend abandoning his intention to take up the Persian slipper.

"Good afternoon, Mycroft," Holmes began. "I confess that I did not expect you so soon."

"Word of Cranmore's release reached Whitehall quickly," was the angry reply. "I suppose I should thank you for your part in this, Sherlock, but otherwise your interference in our affairs has been intolerable."

Holmes gestured that we should all sit, and his brother put aside his top hat and lowered his considerable bulk into the basket chair.

"It is not in my nature to leave a case unfinished," Holmes stated calmly. "nor a problem unsolved, unless they are beyond my abilities."

"But we had the situation well in hand, whether you are aware of it or not."

"Have you then, made adequate arrangements to ensure that our German adversaries, many of whom are still at large, do not interfere with the forthcoming parade?"

Mycroft's expression left me in no doubt that he was unaware that we knew of this, but he hid it quickly. "That is far above your head. All I will say is that their possible presence has been anticipated."

"You have called upon me before. You will recall Mister Melas."

"Yes of course." Holmes' brother produced a gold snuff box and inhaled some of its contents. "But I really cannot allow that to influence things now. I have lost far too many of my people in the course of this affair, without additional complications."

Holmes nodded. "Mr Jude Groat, and others."

"And the latest, the man you knew as Vern Fuller. He had deeply infiltrated the spy ring some time ago but was recently discovered."

If Holmes was surprised by this, as I was, he did not show it.

"Could there be a German sympathiser, in your department?"

"That is doubtful, but I have an extensive review in progress."

"Did you come here today, Mycroft, for any other purpose than to warn me against continuing with this case?" Holmes asked then.

"Only to remind you of the ruthlessness of these people. They may well take action against you and Doctor Watson, especially now."

"Thank you for the warning, but I fear that it comes a little late. There have been attempts, but we are still here."

"Nevertheless, it would be unwise to underestimate their capabilities. Continue to be on your guard."

Mycroft got to his feet with some effort, and we stood also. I was aware that I had not spoken throughout, fearful that I might give something away which my friend would have rather kept from his brother, but now we both wished him good-day and he left.

"Do you think that he might have had another purpose in coming here?" I asked. Holmes watched from the window as Mycroft boarded a hansom.

"Possibly he wished to know how much we had learned during our investigation. It is always difficult to tell with him. I have said before that his abilities are superior to mine."

Before I could reply there came a quick knock on our door and Mrs Hudson entered with a steaming chicken pie. Despite having eaten no more than a few hours ago, I did justice to it easily, while Holmes barely touched his portion.

"Will you accede to your brother's advice?" I enquired as I finished my stewed apple dessert, although I knew the answer already.

Holmes replaced his empty coffee cup. "Hardly. We are uncertain as yet as to the purpose of Colonel Tomkins and his friends, as are Mycroft and his people as far as we know. We must find out the intended route of this procession, however."

"Perhaps the spies intend to assassinate the Maharajah of Tipoor?"

"To what purpose? I cannot see that he stands in the way of the advance of the progress of Imperial Germany."

"Our Queen, then?" I suggested, as appalled at the prospect as I had been before.

"This we have discussed previously, and it is what I have suspected for some time. We must make every effort to ascertain the truth of this, or whatever else is our adversaries' intention."

The following morning we had barely finished breakfast when Holmes leapt from his seat at the table and took up a position near the window.

"Who are you looking for?" I asked as our landlady took away the remains of our meal.

"Anyone who will take a message to the Irregulars."

"You believe that they can discover where the parade is to be held?"

He shook his head, but did not turn away. "No, but they will notice where preparations are being made in advance. Aha!"

With that, he strode past me and descended the stairs quickly. From the window I saw him approach a scruffy urchin and engage him in conversation. Minutes later the lad nodded vigorously and took off at a fast pace. Holmes watched him until he disappeared into the passing crowd, before returning to our room.

"Can you rely on that young man?" I asked him then.

He nodded thoughtfully. "The seed is sown."

I was obliged to visit my practice that morning. A long-standing appointment was kept, advice given and medicine prescribed. On my return I saw that a pile of newspaper cuttings that had awaited insertion into Holmes' index was greatly diminished, and my friend was pacing anxiously from one side of the room to the other.

"You have received no word, then?" I enquired.

"Not as yet."

"Have you eaten?"

"I have asked Mrs Hudson to delay luncheon until your return," he scowled, looking down from the window, "and in anticipation of hearing from the Irregulars. I thought we might inspect the route together, this afternoon."

I took off my hat and coat and seated myself in my usual armchair. "Holmes, the parade is five days from now."

"That is true, but I would have expected the first stages of preparation to be taking place already. It will be necessary to erect barriers and cordon off certain streets in good time, but it appears that I have been premature."

"Perhaps we should return to this tomorrow. What do you say to a walk around the Regents Park, this afternoon?"

To my surprise, and most uncharacteristically, he shrugged off his grim demeanour like a cloak, and suddenly became much brighter.

"You are right of course, old fellow. Nothing is to be gained by descending into melancholia. We do not get out enough, it is true, so we will have our walk." He inclined his head towards the door. "But first I believe I hear our landlady on the stairs."

We had barely begun our meal when the door-bell rang. Our landlady spoke sternly to the caller, whereupon Holmes rose from his seat.

"Continue with your luncheon, Watson. I believe that Mrs Hudson is conversing with a messenger, so I will go down to meet him to avoid incurring her displeasure."

He left the room quickly, so that by the time I had left the table for the half-open window he was already outside. I heard Mrs Hudson return to her quarters, before Holmes spoke to the boy.

"Were you able to discover any preparations in progress?"

The reply was spoken so quietly that I could hear only the occasional word. Holmes nodded several times, and finally reached into his pocket. I saw the glint of coins in the afternoon sun, before the young man saluted and left. Moments later my friend and I resumed our seats.

Holmes said nothing but consumed two mouthfuls of trout, before pushing his plate away.

"They have found something?" I ventured.

"The boy reported that there are signs of preparation in Regent Street, Pall Mall, Trafalgar Square, and parts of Fleet Street, so we now have an indication of the intended route of the procession. I think we will forego the Regents Park for now after all, and examine some likely premises this afternoon. If our German friends intend to disrupt the activities they have to work from close concealment, unless they wish to run a greater risk of discovery."

"It has to be somewhere affording them a clear field of fire. A canon, such as we saw leaving Mendells Lodge, is not hidden easily."

"Precisely. Gregson and his men will of course be searching also, but we will see what can be found."

That afternoon and the next four days were spent searching for likely premises. Holmes seemed to believe that our adversaries would install the canon, if they had not already, somewhere along the route where it could be revealed and fired at the royal coach suddenly. There were two abandoned shops that showed no sign of recent occupation. Other buildings, such as those containing offices, were judged to be too small. A livery stable and a warehouse, situated nearby, showed no signs of recent modification.

"We are approaching the problem from the wrong direction it would seem," Holmes concluded at breakfast on the 27th, "and time is now very short. If we only knew from where Her Majesty will view the procession."

"That information will of course have been withheld. If we leave immediately, we may be able to deduce it from the arrangement of barriers and the facilities prepared for our Queen and the Maharajah. Where a platform has been placed, for example. We can then search again from there."

"You improve constantly, Watson, except that you assume that the attack will come at the viewing site, rather than during the journey to or from it." He made a hopeless gesture. "But you may be right for, despite our best efforts, we have found nothing to indicate the presence of the spies. Gregson and his men will have covered most of the route after us though, and there will be constables in abundance. Nevertheless, we will do as you suggest."

Our early inspection revealed that Her Majesty and the Maharajah were to view the proceedings from an ornate dais now set up at the edge of Trafalgar Square, within sight of the National Gallery, and so we had remained near to watch their arrival. Presently our Queen emerged gracefully from her coach to take up her position. She stood straight, with her head held high, a few feet from her visitor, as cheers erupted from the crowd. The scene altered little until the parade began promptly at ten o'clock. We stood among the assemblage, with Holmes' eyes never still for a second. The first gun-carriages appeared, pulled by horses whose appearance was immaculate. The soldiers of the Royal Artillery rode their mounts proudly, with the brass buttons of their uniforms glinting occasionally in the morning sun. The gun-carriages trundled on and the interest and delight of the Maharajah was evident from his expression which, at this distance, was just discernible.

We were suddenly aware of some disturbance around us, as some of the attending constables began to leave the scene hurriedly to converge nearby. Holmes and I turned to look in another direction, and saw Inspector Gregson pushing his way through the crowd towards us.

"Mr Holmes, Doctor Watson," he began breathlessly. "We have found them. Some officers searching the back streets discovered that a warehouse had been broken into, during the night. They entered and found a group of Germans constructing what looks like a field-gun."

"Excellent work," replied my friend. "What explanation did they give, for their activities?"

"None whatsoever. They would not say a word. As they were handcuffed they simply stood there and watched the constables examine the gun."

"Did it resemble any that we have seen this morning?"

"It did but, Mr Holmes, there was really no danger after all. The condition of the cannon was such that, had they attempted to use it, it would have blown up in their faces. Would you and Doctor Watson care to accompany me, as I interview them?"

"Thank you, Gregson, but I think not," Holmes replied as a confused murmur rippled through the crowd. I think we will stay here with the remainder of your constables, as a precaution against further action. We will join you at the Yard later, if you will permit."

"As you wish." The inspector glanced across to where Her Majesty stood and turned to leave, a little disappointed, I thought, that we had not accompanied him to witness his triumph.

"That is not what we would have expected, Holmes," I remarked as Gregson reached the edge of the crowd.

"Much to the contrary, that is exactly what I would have expected. Surely, Watson, you realise that the men in the warehouse are nothing more than a decoy?"

"It occurred to me immediately that it was a primitive attempt."

"It was no attempt at all, old fellow. Merely a device to attract as many of the official force as possible away from here. The parade is almost at an end now, so they have little time left."

We continued to watch until the last of the gun-carriages appeared. Further along the route, possibly as far ahead as Fleet Street, something must have occurred because the parade came to a sudden halt. I had an impression of a party of burly men who had remained in the background, closing in to protect Her Majesty and the Maharajah. The remaining constables, spaced out before us, began to look around suspiciously.

Holmes reviewed the scene and moved at once. "Quickly, Watson."

We pushed forward, striving to pass through the crowd and approach the procession. The reason for my friend's alarm came to me then: the final gun carriage, with more uniformed horsemen in its wake, had come to a halt almost directly before our Queen!

Holmes reached the road, attracting wary looks from both the horsemen and the group who surrounded Her Majesty. I emerged from the crowd after him, feeling rather foolish and unsure as to what action to take.

A strange silence seemed to descend upon us. One of the horses became restless and was calmed by its rider. Holmes and the soldiers stared at each other for an instant, before he pointed to the one nearest the gun-carriage.

A constable, probably confused as to what was taking place, pushed his way through the crowd and Holmes called to him as he emerged nearby: "Arrest that man at once!"

Before the officer could move, the soldier who my friend had indicated spurred his horse forward. He drew his sword, ready to slash at anyone attempting to impede his escape, and rode away at a furious pace. All eyes were on him as he tore towards Fleet Street, and I saw shock and incomprehension written on many faces. Almost unseen, a small man emerged from the crowd and approached the forsaken gun-carriage. Something flared in his hands and he hurried forward, to be stopped abruptly by an uppercut from Holmes. I rushed to his side and attempted to stamp out the burning mass that had fallen to the ground. Then the scene became confused, as panic beset the crowd.

Chapter 14 – The Reckoning

I have retained no recollection of the time, but at least two hours must have passed, before Holmes and I found ourselves at Scotland Yard, in the office of Inspector Gregson.

Already, the hysteria of the crowd, the mad horseman and my last impression of our Queen and the Maharajah being escorted from their positions, were a confused blur in my mind. Holmes' actions were a mystery to me also.

"Well, Mr Holmes," Gregson began as he placed his hands before him on his desk, "I trust you can explain your conduct."

Holmes sat upright in his chair.   "I will be glad to do so, Inspector. As you saw, the parade had almost ended and it seemed likely that any attempts at disruption would take place soon, since there was little time left. When the procession came to an unexpected halt I suspected at once that this was planned, especially as the last gun-carriage was positioned so very near our Queen."

"That was why you left the crowd and approached the soldiers?"

"Indeed. At first it was solely because I had noticed minute differences between the final cannon and those that had gone before. As I drew closer I realised that the horseman was none other than the German spy we know as Colonel Tomkins."

"Gregson looked mildly astonished. "And how, may I ask, did you deduce that?"

"His face, of course, was all but obscured by the helmet he wore. Nevertheless, his moustache was visible."

"His *moustache?*"

"You are doubtless aware that the Prussian style is quite different from that usually approved for our own forces."

"And how do you account for this man's presence there?" The inspector appeared slightly embarrassed, probably because the intensive search by the official force had been fruitless.

"I cannot, since I am not privy to their scheme." Holmes looked away, distracted momentarily by a door slamming further along the corridor. "But I can tell you this, Inspector. You will find, if you have not done so already, the body of the man whom Colonel Tomkins replaced. Somewhere, a soldier lies bound and gagged, or worse."

"That discovery has already occurred. The poor fellow's throat was cut."

"My condolences to his family." My friend's expression deepened for a moment. "Doubtlessly, the horse was found wandering in or near Fleet Street."

Gregson nodded. "But what of the man you assaulted? What part does he play in this?"

"He must be an extremely patriotic soul, to be willing to give up his life so easily."

Inspector Gregson and I exchanged puzzled glances, before Holmes continued.

"The cannon was not a gun at all, but an explosive device. It was fashioned in the likeness of a field-gun in order to guarantee its approach to our Queen undetected. The fellow I attacked was in the process of applying a tube of burning phosphorus to a specially-designed vent which would have immediately ignited the internal fuse, hence the heavy gloves he wore. I imagine the resulting explosion would certainly have seen the end of our sovereign, as well as the Maharajah and much of the crowd, as well as the soldiers and their mounts. An examination of the device will doubtlessly confirm this."

"As regards our Queen and the visiting Maharajah, they had been installed in a place of safety before the parade began. The volunteers who substituted for them were an excellent likeness, I thought." Gregson's expression did not change, he offered no praise for Holmes' actions, but I imagine he felt the same sensations of horror as myself on learning of this monstrous plot. The severity he had shown towards Holmes and myself lightened a little. "How did you define the true nature of the cannon, Mr Holmes?" he asked then.

"I suspected something of the sort previously, since nothing had been found or transpired to suggest that firing was to take place during the procession. As I recognised Colonel Tomkins I was able to peer into the barrel which was blocked to prevent the explosive force from dispersing normally."

"We are questioning the man who attempted to ignite the fuse, but he has told us nothing. I am expecting your brother's agents to arrive shortly, so we have little time. Are you aware of the whereabouts of any remaining members of the spy ring, Mr Holmes?"

"I am sorry, Gregson, but I cannot help you there. However, we must not lose sight of the fact that Colonel

Tomkins, or Herr Hans Veidermann as he really is, is still at large."

The inspector was silent for what seemed a long time.

"Very well," he said at last. "I think there is nothing more I need ask of you, for now. However, there may be more questions soon."

Holmes and I rose, as he answered. "We will be at Baker Street, Inspector, should you need us."

"Were you aware of the substitution, Holmes?" I asked as we hailed a cab.

"Oh, yes." He informed the driver of our destination and climbed in after me. "The brave lady who presented herself as our sovereign was slightly taller, and carried herself differently. As for the Maharajah, I could not tell since I have never seen the gentleman, but I imagine that one of his entourage was substituted for him."

I cast my mind back to the crowd, the soldiers and their narrowly-averted destruction. "Doubtlessly, we will be hearing from Inspector Gregson again, before long."

There, I was in error. As it was, we heard nothing more from Scotland Yard for the next two weeks. No word came from Mycroft also, which relieved my friend somewhat since he anticipated another lecture of disapproval. Holmes seemed to have put the case from his mind now that the danger to our Queen was averted, and mentioned only once that he expected Colonel Tomkins would reappear at some future time.

During an evening soon after, we found ourselves in an evil-smelling alley in Limehouse, having just concluded the affair which I will one day publish as 'The Adventure of the

Devil's Bride'. Thirty yards ahead was a thoroughfare where we would certainly have found a hansom to convey us back to our lodgings, had not a figure appeared out of the shadows to stand in the baleful light of a street lamp.

The evening fog was thick, and swirled about the man like smoke. As we drew closer his form took shape, and his top hat and dark clothes became clearer. He barred our way, unmoving.

I looked back, over my shoulder. "Holmes, there are two more behind us, advancing quickly."

"Are you armed, Watson?"

"I had not thought it necessary, tonight."

"Neither did I. Let us see if these gentlemen intend to accost us."

We reached the end of the alley with the figure before us not having moved. In the meagre light I could make out a clean-shaven face that I did not recognise, but when he spoke I knew him at once.

"Good evening, Mr Sherlock Holmes. We are fortunate, I think, in finding your companion also."

"We meet again, Colonel Tomkins," Holmes did not sound surprised. "I see that you have taken measures to alter your appearance."

"Indeed. But Colonel Tomkins is no more. I am myself again. My name is Hans Veidermann, as I am sure you have discovered, by now." His accent was more discernible than I remembered, as if reverting to his true self had affected it.

"Very well," Holmes said. "What is it to be now, Herr Veidermann?"

A grim smile spread over the German's face. "A reckoning of sorts, I think. I have reported to my superiors, and they have made it clear to me that they would very much like to interview you both. We are to take you to a place where someone is to arrive to conduct the proceedings, which will progress regardless of any resistance from you. I believe the intension is to learn something of your remarkable skills of detection, Mr Holmes, and in particular how they were employed against us recently."

I sensed that the men following now stood a few feet behind us. At this moment, I reflected that the reassuring weight of my service weapon in my pocket would have been exceedingly welcome. But as I glanced back again I saw that the light from the lamp glinted on their revolvers, which were held steady and aimed at Holmes and myself. The faces of the two figures were hidden by the shadow beneath the brims of their top hats.

"There is little I can tell you, and still less that I would." my friend said.

"Oh, but I am sure that is true." Herr Veidermann glanced at me, briefly. "I know that you will be most reluctant to co-operate, but the sight of Doctor Watson in distress may change that somewhat."

Holmes merely shrugged, as if accepting the inevitable.

"So, gentlemen," our adversary said as a carriage appeared, "as soon as we have ascertained that you are not armed, we can set off."

He made a signal to his comrades and they advanced with their weapons aimed at our stomachs. We had no choice but to submit to a quick search of our persons, and the coach was soon speeding along the deserted streets with us under constant and silent scrutiny.

After a while I grew impatient with the silence and made to speak, but in the poor light Holmes silenced me instantly with a glare.

We made our way through the fog at a dangerous pace. The driver constantly whipped up the horses, urging the poor beasts on although the way ahead was hidden. Much time seemed to pass before the coach was brought to a halt and we were ordered to alight. I could now smell the Thames, but the fog prevented me from identifying our surroundings. The air was dank and the silence broken by an occasional shout or fragment of speech from unseen persons, as the glow of lamps appeared and passed briefly along the river.

Herr Veidermann gave sharp orders in his native language, and his comrades took up positions behind us. He led the way through the fog and brought us to a halt on a flat, stone-flagged area. The smell of the river was stronger here, and I could hear the ripples against the bank.

"We will not be kept waiting for long," our captor said.

Presently a faint glow appeared close by. It grew in intensity until we could make out the indistinct shape of a steam launch.

"Prepare to board."

Holmes and I did so with gun barrels pressed against our backs. Soon we all stood on the deck, barely able to see the receding landing-stage as it was enveloped by the fog. We became aware that several of the crew had joined us, though they were unarmed. One, glaring at us, was particularly noticeable - a towering giant with a scarred face.

It came to me that Holmes had accepted the situation with exceptional calm. Since Herr Veidermann had announced his plans for us I had fought hard to contain my increasing dread. Yet my friend seemed strangely unaffected so that I wondered whether, as on past occasions, he had already formed a plan of escape. I glanced again through the drifting fog at the roughs who surrounded us, and thought it doubtful, if not impossible. I felt that his optimism was unrealistic, that in reality we were doomed.

After a while the launch came to rest somewhere in mid-stream. The hatch opened and a tall man whose days of youth were well behind him appeared from below. He was dressed formally, his top hat and black cloak creating a sinister appearance, and his expression was grim as he surveyed the scene silently.

Our captors were immediately respectful, standing stiffly to attention with much clicking of heels. Herr Veidermann then stood to one side to give his superior an unobstructed view.

He turned to speak to us, triumph written on his face. "Allow me to introduce Herr Spengler. At least, that is the name we will use here. It is not necessary, gentlemen, that you should be aware of the real identity of your inquisitor, only that you should answer his questions truthfully. I recommend that you do so."

At his gesture, two crewmen advanced on us with the apparent intention of forcing us to a position more convenient for what was to occur. One of them pushed Holmes savagely and struck at him with some sort of club, only to be cast over the side by the use of the Oriental method of combat that my friend had once described to me as that used to despatch Professor Moriarty.

I heard the crewman splash into the water, and saw some surprised glances exchanged, but no attempt was made to retrieve him.

'I did not order an attack,' Herr Spengler said. 'He has paid the price for his disobedience."

I had expected immediate repercussions, but our captors looked at Holmes with a new respect. The other crewman stood back, now more wary.

Herr Spengler took a pace towards us. I felt the boat move as a slight swell took it, and a moment of silence followed. I saw now strands of iron-grey hair protruding from beneath his hat, and eyes that glared pitilessly. Without looking away, he addressed the crewman standing nearby after handing him a pistol.

"I shall now ask certain questions of this man," he indicated Holmes. "If he refuses to answer, or if he displays deceit, I will raise my hand in a signal. You will then fire at his companion, beginning with his lower legs and progressing upwards with each further indication. Is that clear?"

The crewman saluted and acknowledged at once. I saw that the brutish man with the scarred face had also drawn close, doubtlessly in anticipation of any further violent resistance.

"Very well, we will begin," our interrogator said then. "Mr Holmes, how did you manage to penetrate our organisation?"

"There is no mystery to that," Holmes replied. "If one observes, looks for indications and watches for the errors of ones adversaries, much can be learned."

"But, specifically?"

"Herr Veidermann's portrayal of an English colonel was transparent. I was extremely surprised that our authorities had allowed such a charade to continue."

Herr Spengler looked away for an instant, giving his subordinate a black and deadly look. Had it not been for the poor light, I felt sure that I would have seen the colour drain from Herr Veidermann's face.

Lights appeared, shining out of the fog and steadily advancing. Another steam launch passed close, causing our craft to tilt so that most of us stumbled to one side as we reached for the hand-rail.

"There must be more, Mr Holmes," Herr Spengler glanced at the crewman standing with his pistol at the ready, as the launch steadied. "You must speak. It would be unwise to try my patience further."

Holmes nodded. "I have tried to convey to you that I am in no way an agent of my government. I have no authority or special powers of any kind. I merely analyse and act upon my observations."

"It seems that I must remind you of the consequences of wasting my time." Herr Spengler turned to the armed crewman. "Heinrich, you are an excellent shot. Demonstrate to

Mr Holmes and Doctor Watson the precision of which you are capable."

The pistol was aimed at my feet and fired immediately, the report dull in the enclosing fog. I gritted my teeth, waiting for the pain of smashed bone and torn flesh. I felt nothing and, looking down in surprise, made out a small hole in the deck no more than half an inch away from my boot. I exhaled with temporary relief.

"You will receive no further warning," Herr Spengler assured us. "So unless you wish to see your friend die slowly, Mr Holmes, you will speak now."

I glanced at Holmes, who appeared to be distracted by an examination of our immediate surroundings. I noted that Heinrich and the two men who had accompanied Herr Veidermann were the only ones holding firearms. Three other crewmen held clubs, probably belaying-pins. The scarred giant had retreated almost to the hatch entrance and was reaching for something apparently concealed near there. Because the launch had tilted with the passing of the other craft, everyone stood much more closely together.

"I agree, Herr Spengler," Holmes said then. "The time to speak has indeed arrived." He raised his head so that his voice would carry. "I think we have had enough of this, Fenwick."

Incomprehension was written on every face, as it must have been on mine. Of my friend's apparently unconnected remark I had no understanding, until I saw that the large crewman with the scarred face had slowly altered his position to the edge of the group and now confronted it with a heavy-gauge shotgun.

"Throw your pistol down," he ordered Heinrich in very English tones," and you two gentlemen near the rail would be well advised to do this also."

At a nod from Herr Spengler, the weapons clattered to the deck. One of the crewmen took a quick step forward, but stopped as Fenwick raised his shotgun further.

"Calm yourself, old fellow," Holmes advised me as he took a police whistle from his pocket.

A moment later, its shrill tones filled the night air.

Chapter 15 – Almost a Conclusion

The wail of the whistle seemed restricted by the wall of fog. I wondered, as we waited, if it had been heard. Silence descended again, and I inspected our prisoners as best I could.

Herr Spengler wore a philosophical expression, perhaps already planning how he would proceed if Holmes' signal for help went unanswered. The two men who had brought us here with Herr Veidermann looked in his direction, awaiting orders. I saw that the remaining crewmen seemed undecided as to whether they should brave the shotgun in an attempt to regain control. Fenwick appeared to sense this, and smiled grimly as he shook his head.

It was Herr Veidermann who surprised me. He had taken on a wild look, and it came to me that he must be fearfully considering his future. Remembering his superior's apparent response to Holmes' critical remark, I concluded that his choice between capture or returning to his own land was not a pleasant one.

Holmes gave a further blast of his whistle.

"We should not have to wait long," he told Fenwick.

Almost at the same moment I heard the approach of another craft. Very soon green lamps became visible through the curtain of fog. A police launch appeared and pulled up alongside before four burly constables leapt from it, armed and ready to take charge. I saw a look of disappointment cross Herr Spengler's face.

"Ah, good evening, Inspector Gregson," Holmes said jubilantly as the official detective clambered aboard. "As you see, we have a sizeable catch for you tonight."

Gregson scowled. "We would have been here sooner, but for this accursed fog."

"No matter. If you would be so good as to convey these gentlemen to the cells at Scotland Yard, I am sure that my brother will send word in the morning."

"My superiors have warned against questioning them. Apparently that pleasure is reserved for those well above my rank."

"Possibly, but do not allow that to disappoint you. These are enemies of our country who will be dealt with accordingly. I will ensure that your part in this will not go unrecognised."

"Thank you, Mr Holmes." Gregson then gestured to the constables. Shortly afterwards began a procession of the handcuffed prisoners to board the police launch. One of the crewman stumbled during the transfer and Herr Veidermann broke loose, taking advantage of the momentary diversion.

Despite his manacles, he threw himself from the deck of the police launch. I listened for the splash as he entered the water, but the fog had hidden the boat's proximity to the bank and, the Thames being narrower here, he landed upon a deserted wharf.

Apparently uninjured, he began a frantic run, with several of the constables discharging their weapons as he disappeared into the fog. We heard, but could not see, a coach somewhere in the darkness. The abrupt ceasing of the sounds of the horses' hooves suggested that the conveyance had been reined in suddenly, before a scream pierced the night air. Holmes leapt onto the jetty followed by Gregson, but they were too late. The noise of the coach being driven away at speed reached our ears as the constables fired again, aimlessly it seemed to me, until we heard the wrenching of tortured wood as it was forced to take a sharp corner at too fast a pace.

I followed my friend and the inspector as there came a tremendous splash and the beasts, unharmed, were revealed as they pulled the broken shafts behind them before the constables brought them to a halt. The three of us hurried to the spot where we judged the coach to have left the bank but, even though the fog cleared for a moment, there was nothing to be seen.

"The body will likely be retrieved a mile or so further down, if the current holds," Gregson said as we turned away.

We learned later that the body of the coachman was found on the narrow path as the fog cleared. The poor fellow's neck was broken, and it was apparent that he had been thrown to the ground in Herr Veidermann's desperation to escape.

It was well into the early hours when Holmes and I finally retired. He proved to be infuriatingly reticent at breakfast next morning, but by the time we had finished our coffee I could contain my curiosity and impatience no longer.

"Holmes," I began as we settled ourselves in our usual armchairs, "will you kindly explain to me how the conclusion to the events of last night came about?"

He leaned back in his chair, smiling at my frustration. "Very well, Watson, if you insist. I confess to harbouring some anxiety, as we were taken aboard that launch. It was when I recognised Fenwick, that the reason for Mycroft's insistence that we distance ourselves from this affair became clear to me."

"It was because Herr Spengler's branch of the organisation had already been infiltrated?"

"Precisely. Fenwick, a former actor, is one of my brother's most capable agents. I met him briefly some time ago, when I called at Whitehall in connection with another matter."

"But how did the police launch come to be on hand?"

"Fenwick explained to me later that he had attained a trusted position within the spy ring. He communicated their movements and other information to Mycroft's office whenever he could. On learning the purpose of Herr Spengler's river excursion he reported the details, enabling his colleagues to notify Scotland Yard to send out the craft that rescued us. I think Gregson would have dearly liked to question the prisoners himself, but his orders forbade it. By now they will be in more skilful hands, but it is regretful that the man we knew as Colonel Tomkins will not be among them."

I nodded. "Has the body of Herr Veidermann been recovered?"

"I read the early edition of *The Standard* before you joined me. The body was washed up more than a mile distant. It was already the worse for the attention of rats, I fear."

"A horrible and disgusting prospect, yet I cannot bring myself to feel pity."

"I find it difficult to imagine that he would have felt any for us, had our positions been reversed." Holmes had appeared increasingly restless, during our discussion. Now he rose and crossed the room to peer through the window. "However, as you have doubtless realised, this affair is not over as yet."

I considered, thinking back briefly. "The daughter of Mr and Mrs Cranmore?"

"Precisely. I informed Gregson as to the circumstances since, surprisingly, the member of parliament did not mention his offspring's predicament at the time of his rescue. The inspector has telegraphed to Norfolk with a view to causing the local police to organise a search."

"Let us hope that they are quickly successful. Their familiarity with the area should prove to be of considerable advantage."

After apparently seeing nothing of interest outside, he turned to face me. "Perhaps, but I cannot but feel that to leave it to them would be to allow this case to remain unfinished. I told Gregson as much, and he grudgingly agreed to request the local constabulary to be agreeable to our own enquiry. If you would make your arrangements, Watson, I would be exceedingly glad to have your company on an excursion to Norfolk. Unless you have other plans, of course."

"I am with you, as ever," I smiled. "A short telegram will ensure that my practice is maintained.

"Capital!" Holmes picked up a pad from the desk and handed it to me. "Pray attend to that without delay for, unless I am mistaken, there is a train at two o'clock that will get us to our destination by this evening."

It was in fact almost eight o'clock when the local train, the connection from the London express, drew into the tiny

Norfolk station of Little Curlingham. The place appeared deserted save for the station master, who lay sprawled behind his desk in a deep sleep. We noticed with distaste the profusion of empty whisky bottles, strewed untidily across the floor.

"Our train driver is apparently familiar with the situation here," Holmes remarked, "since he continued without the usual signal."

"That fellow should be reported. His drunkenness could cause considerable difficulty to the railway and its passengers, even accidents."

"Quite so," Holmes agreed, "although I do not believe that much traffic passes through here. It seems an isolated place."

I nodded. "How are we to get to the village?"

"I believe we are obliged to walk."

We were about to leave by the gate at the end of the platform, when we were confronted by an elderly man dragging two milk churns in his wake. Holmes asked him if it were possible, when all the churns had been delivered, for us to ride with him in his cart into the village."

He gave us a shifty look. "I don't think so, sirs. Its right out of my way, you see."

"But for a half-sovereign, it would not delay your return to your farm overmuch, surely?"

"It would be an inconvenience," he said, before reading in Holmes' expression that the offer would not be increased, "but I suppose I could spare you gentlemen the walk. Climb up on the cart, then."

It did not take us long to realise, during the journey that turned out to be less than a mile, that the direct route to our driver's farm passed through Little Curlingham. I confess to feeling a flush of anger at being so deceived, but my companion wore a faint smile and said nothing. Presently, we arrived at the outskirts of the village. A church with a crooked spire was in darkness, as were many of the cottages. I remembered that Holmes also had sent a telegram, when I despatched the message to my locum to inform him of my delayed return. I had assumed, apparently correctly, that it was to reserve rooms for us. We alighted in a dark street near a row of shops, all with blinds drawn. As the cart turned a corner and was lost to our sight, I noticed that the only sounds of activity came from a well-lit tavern ahead.

"The Country House Inn," Holmes proclaimed as if had read my mind. "They will be prepared for us, I think."

The landlord, a fat and jovial fellow with a patch over one eye, welcomed us effusively. He remarked that travellers to this village were infrequent, and showed us to two clean and acceptable rooms on an upper floor before offering a supper of local trout.

"Pray accompany the food with a pint of your best ale for each of us," Holmes requested. "Thank you, landlord. We will be down directly."

The meal was excellent and we drank and talked for a while afterwards, until our host passed our table carrying a tray of empty glasses. Holmes caught his attention and asked the whereabouts of the local police station, raising his voice to overcome the clamour at the bar from the crowd of farm-workers and others who were obviously regulars here.

The landlord's single eye narrowed. "There's only one in a village of this size of course, sir. You'll find it in Greatmoor Street, next to the saddler's shop." He half-turned away, and then paused with a concerned expression. "There's no trouble is there, sir?"

"None at all," Holmes said lightly. "We are just hoping to renew an old acquaintance."

The smile reappeared on the landlord's face and he enquired as to our further needs. My friend answered that we were tired after a long journey and intended to return to our rooms. The man wished us goodnight and continued with his duties.

We ascended the stairs again, and on the landing Holmes warned that we most likely had a busy day before us tomorrow. Shortly afterwards I lay awaiting sleep and listening to him pacing, presumably because he was turning the situation over in his mind or was as yet uncertain as to how we should proceed. We had met with resistance from the official force locally, many times and in many places, before now.

Our landlord was no less jovial at breakfast, which was of rashers of ham and fried eggs. Holmes and I left for Greatmoor Street as soon as we had eaten our fill, and had little difficulty in finding the police station. It was a building of grey stone, and forbidding appearance.

We entered to be confronted by a thick-set man with an immaculately trimmed beard. His sergeant's uniform, I noticed, was well-pressed.

He regarded us suspiciously before politely asking our business, whereupon Holmes furnished a much shortened account of events in London.

"You will have received a telegram from Inspector Gregson of Scotland Yard, regarding our purpose here," he finished.

The sergeant looked at us without expression. "We are but a small community here, and so a small station. I am the senior officer, Sergeant Redfern, and I have two constables, Lyntley and Martin. It is a rare occasion when we need help with our duties, but when we do a member of the detective branch in Norwich is usually sent. We require no further assistance."

"I take it then, that you have already made enquiries regarding the missing girl," Holmes replied.

"We have noticed nothing that could suggest that she is being held within our jurisdiction. No strangers have appeared hereabouts, and such an abduction would certainly be carried out by such, since we harbour no criminals around here." He paused and glanced at the olive painted walls and the board containing public notices, perhaps wondering how best to dismiss us. "Why, I've known almost everyone in the village, since I was a young 'un."

Two constables appeared from a corridor, placing their helmets on their heads as they prepared to leave the building. We glanced at them and Sergeant Redfern acknowledged their departure.

"You will not object then, if we conduct our own investigation? I am anxious to assure Scotland Yard that we can exclude this part of the country from any further enquiries."

The sergeant nodded. "You must do as you please of course but, since we have seen nothing to indicate otherwise, I am certain that the abducted girl has been taken far away from her school, and well out of this district. Assuredly, there has been no one who could be thought of as a countryman of Herr Veidermann anywhere around here. Had there been, we would doubtlessly have known."

To my surprise, Holmes sighed and gave a disinterested shrug of his shoulders. "Very well, Sergeant. Our thanks to you for simplifying our enquiry. Since there seems little for us to occupy ourselves with in the light of your information, I think we will spend a few days in and around your charming village before returning to London. Good-day to you."

Back in the street once more, we passed the saddler's shop and the tobacconists which was also the newsagent's shop, before I spoke to my friend.

"That was not very helpful, Holmes. I am sorry to have contributed nothing to the discussion."

"Much to the contrary, old fellow, I am exceedingly glad that you remained silent. As soon as I saw that the local representative of the official force objected to our presence, I was glad to be able to study him without distraction. However, his final remark confirmed much that I suspected.

He is hiding something from us. It may be that it is simply that he sees us as an interference where he believes that none is necessary, or it may be something more. We shall see before long, I think."

His stride was purposeful, and I could not imagine how he intended to proceed.

"Where are we bound for now?"

"The Post Office," he replied as we crossed to the other side of the street.

Holmes quickly despatched a telegram, and we adjourned to a corner coffee-house.

"I have told the Postmistress that we will return shortly," he said as cups of a steaming brew were placed before us. "She will surely receive an answer before long."

"The message was to Gregson, of course." I ventured.

"Indeed. You will recall that I alluded to a remark of Sergeant Redfern's that aroused my curiosity. He mentioned the true identity of Colonel Tomkins. Knowing something of Inspector Gregson's hesitancy in sharing information, I cannot imagine him confiding this to the sergeant in his telegram. He is much more likely to have alerted him to the likelihood of the kidnapped girl being held in this area and to our impending arrival, but nothing more."

"How then, assuming that your supposition is correct, could Sergeant Redfern possibly know this? It is most unlikely that the local newspapers would have received a full account from their London counterparts so soon."

Holmes nodded. "Precisely. You see then, why I believe that something is amiss here. I think we will order another cup of this excellent coffee, and by the time our cups are empty the Postmistress may have something for us."

Inspector Gregson had been prompt with his reply. Holmes thanked the Postmistress as he accepted the form and glanced at it briefly.

"As I thought," he said.

"Then are we to return to the station to confront the sergeant?"

He shook his head. "I think not. I propose that we return to the inn for lunch, before spending the afternoon acquainting ourselves with the streets and lanes of this rather picturesque village. When that is done, there will doubtless be time for a brandy before we change for dinner. Afterwards we will observe the police station unseen, until the first of the officers finishes his shift. Then we will follow until he reaches his home, which we will watch until the early hours. You see, Watson, if one of these men is somehow connected to the spy ring by his participation in Miss Cranmore's abduction, he will be anxious to tell whoever is holding her of our arrival. When he ventures out to do this, we will be close behind."

"So you are not convinced of Sergeant Redfern's guilt, despite his remark?"

"Not completely. He could have heard the name from one of his colleagues, and been ignorant of its significance. As you concluded, the full facts of the events in the capital are unlikely to be known here yet."

We passed the time as Holmes had suggested. By the time darkness fell we had already installed ourselves in the deep gateway of a builders yard, some way along the street from the police station. I had thought that the distance might complicate our observation, causing it to be difficult to see the departure of the sergeant or his officers, but after a while an overhead lamp was lit, bathing the entrance in a pool of light.

"I had considered enquiring of the landlord as to whether a cart is available for hire," my friend whispered from the shadows, "but I have since concluded that each man is likely to live within walking distance of his employment. You will have noticed that the station has only one entrance, and there was no sign of bicycles within."

Before I could reply, a shadow fell across the entrance to the station. Holmes placed a hand on my shoulder to ensure that I could not move or make a sound until the striding figure had passed us and vanished out of our sight.

"Now," he whispered. "Do not speak until he has reached his destination. Follow my movements closely."

We then emerged from our hiding-place, quickly closing the distance as our quarry took several turns through the poorly-lit streets. Not for the first time, I was astounded at Holmes' skill in hiding our pursuit. As we drew nearer he seemed able to anticipate exactly when Sergeant Redfern, for we could now clearly see that it was he, would glance back, and to guide us into doorways, entrance passages or any other place of concealment that presented itself.

Presently the streets were left behind, and the houses became fewer. To remain unseen, should the sergeant turnabout, was now impossible, though my companion did not hesitate to continue. I was relieved when a vastly overgrown bush at the side of the lane provided shelter, just as the officer turned into a short path leading to a whitewashed cottage.

"We are fortunate," Holmes said in a low voice. "That great oak is almost opposite to the sergeant's house. We can observe safely, from there."

As we concealed ourselves behind the thick trunk, a lamp was lit in the upper floor of the cottage and curtains were drawn.

"He has retired," I said unnecessarily. "It does not seem that he will leave his house tonight."

"Nevertheless, we will remain for a while. It is as well to make certain."

"How long would be sufficient, do you think?"

"At least until the early hours."

I stifled a yawn. "Then if he has any such business to conduct, let us hope he does so promptly."

"Indeed. I would expect him to report our intervention to his accomplices at the first opportunity, so it is likely that it is necessary to maintain this vigil for tonight only. There is another possibility, however."

"Have I missed something?"

"That is possible," I could not see his expression as the light went out, leaving only a distant roadside lamp to illuminate the scene, "unless you have considered that he may have a regular appointment with a visitor. That is unlikely, but it is a further reason for us to remain."

"Of course, but if nothing occurs I presume we are to concentrate on the sergeant's colleagues?"

In the dim glow, Holmes pulled his ear-flapped travelling cap more firmly onto his head. "We

must. One of them is somehow connected to the London spy ring. Miss Cranmore's life may depend upon our success."

Chapter 16 – Who is the Spy?

The hours passed slowly. The monotony of our vigil was disturbed only once, when an aged figure stumbled past the cottage and paused to give voice to a selection of oaths in the direction of the sergeant's bedroom window before continuing along the lane.

"From the content of that little speech," Holmes murmured in the darkness, "I would conclude that the fellow has a considerable history of arrests, probably for his actions while in the inebriated state he enjoys at the moment."

"At first I thought our patience was about to be rewarded."

"I dismissed the notion, as I realised that he could hardly maintain his balance."

Shortly after, my friend decided that nothing more was likely to occur. We returned to the inn to find it locked up for the night, but to awaken the landlord proved unnecessary when Holmes used his pick-lock to gain our admittance. Nothing stirred as we crept to our rooms, and I slept soundly until disturbed by the sounds of activity from below.

"Today our task has intensified," Holmes explained during breakfast, "for we do not know at what hour the remaining officers will leave the station. I fear that we have little choice but to return to our hiding-place nearby."

As it happened, this proved unnecessary. Holmes led us on a circuitous route, doubtlessly to avoid passing the police station, and we were in a different thoroughfare near a cart-horse stable when he suddenly turned to me.

"Enter the passage ahead. Do it quickly."

I complied at once, with some puzzlement. "What is it, Holmes?"

He looked out from the narrow alley, across the street. "The fellow in a green pea-coat, striding urgently along. He looks different when not in uniform, but that is Constable Lyntley."

"I believe you are correct, although I confess that I had not noticed." I peered in the direction that he had indicated. "He must have worked the night shift."

"Undoubtedly, before hurriedly returning home to change his clothes. You will notice how he often looks around as if concerned that he might be pursued. I am curious about this, Watson, and it may be as well to resume our investigation here."

We followed the constable, with Holmes employing his skills as before, into a short street where many of the houses showed some neglect. A carriage waited for its owner, outside an address that I judged to be a house of ill-repute, providing convenient cover from which we observed our quarry knock at a door opposite before being scrutinized and eventually admitted.

"He was most careful to ensure that he was not followed or observed before entering," I remarked. "Perhaps we have found the place of Miss Cranmore's confinement."

"Possibly, but observe the suspicious glances from the occupants of the neighbouring houses. Clearly, it is common knowledge that something out of the ordinary transpires there, but I cannot think that the unlawful imprisonment of a young lady would go unreported for long, especially as a reward has been promised for any relevant information. As we see, two more have just entered the house under the watchful eye of a woman who sits knitting in the window of that rather dilapidated place nearby which was once, if the badly painted-out signs on the wall are to be believed, a grocer's shop. A word with her, I think, might be informative."

We approached the house, which was a mere few yards away, and Holmes knocked the door but once before the woman left her post at the window and answered.

"What be you gentlemen wanting?" she enquired curiously.

"We are conducting an assimilation of the properties hereabouts, on behalf of the District Council," Holmes said with an air of authority. "It is quite clear that some of these houses are more than residential. Can you, for instance, confirm that the address where the gentleman in a top hat has just been admitted, is regularly used for religious meetings?"

The woman threw up her arms, laughing loudly. "You've got that one wrong, sir, that you have. All sorts come and go there, day and night, and we've known around here for a long time that gambling goes on. There's fights sometimes, when the losers can't pay their debts. It's terrible, the noise when one's trying to sleep, I can tell you."

"We will report this. Doubtlessly something will be done about it, before long." Holmes thanked the woman, and we left.

Fortunately, a workman's tea-shop was situated near the end of the street. Holmes ensured that we sat at a table near the window as we eventually consumed a scant luncheon, with a good view of the house where Constable Lyntley had spent most of the morning.

"It seems as if the constable has become involved rather extensively," he remarked. "We will give further consideration to him, later. As for now, another visit to the station may be appropriate. I would welcome the opportunity to interview Constable Martin, if Sergeant Redfern will permit it."

Not unexpectedly, the sergeant was not pleased by our presence.

"I had thought that you would have departed the village by now, Mr Holmes," he said in grim answer to my friend's request. "In any case, what you ask cannot be. Constable Martin has not attended to take up his duties today, and it is my intention to send Constable Lyntley out to discover the cause." He glanced at the clock, high on the wall above us. "That is, if Lyntley would condescend to arrive on time. I will be having words with him too, before this day is out."

"There is a question I would ask, if you would be so good."

Sergeant Redfern leaned forward, faintly exasperated, across the tall reception desk. "If I can, sir."

"Do you recall mentioning, during our previous visit, the name of a certain German who was involved in recent events in the capital?"

He spent a moment in consideration, before nodding. "Herr Veidermann, I think it was."

"Quite so. How did it come about, that you knew that name?"

"Why, I think," he looked surprised at the question, "that it was Constable Martin who said it in conversation. How he came by it, I do not know."

"I take it that reports of the incident have yet to reach here, or you would have been able to explain your knowledge at once."

For the first time, the sergeant took on an uncertain look. "You are correct, Mr Holmes, we have heard nothing officially, as yet. How then, could Martin have known?"

"Perhaps by means of a telegram from associates in London. It has been apparent from the first that someone here is connected, possibly as an accomplice, with the spy ring that was exposed there. The situation you see, Sergeant, has now become urgent, since the abductors of the girl who I originally consulted you about will certainly wish to avoid being identified by her if she were rescued."

I shuddered at the thought.

"You mean they are likely to murder her?" the policeman queried.

"If they have not done so already. You see that it is vital that we find her quickly?"

"Of course. Perhaps there is something in what you say, after all." Sergeant Redfern paused suddenly, and looked past us. "But here is Constable Lyntley, now."

The constable, now in uniform once more, entered the station at a quick pace. Breathless, he began to offer excuses for his lateness, but Sergeant Redfern cut him short.

"I will speak to you later, Lyntley. You will go at once to the home of Constable Martin and bring him here, unless he is bedridden. If that is so then return here and I will visit his home myself, later." He made a dismissive gesture. "Set off at once."

I spoke for the first time, risking Holmes' disapproval.

"Sergeant, might Mr Holmes and myself accompany the constable?"

Despite everything, my words were received with indecision. "That would be irregular, and we frown upon interference from the public, but you are free to do as you please."

Constable Martin, it transpired, lived alone in a red brick building near the edge of the village. Again we maintained a fast pace along the cobbled streets and across the village green, during which Holmes made no mention of Constable Lyntley's earlier activities, but explained to him the nature of our suspicions.

The constable's expression darkened. "Germans, you say? I suppose the name 'Martin' could be from that country, as well as ours. Who would ever have thought it?"

"Nothing is proven, as yet." I pointed out.

We reached a short lane not far from the dairy, thick with trees and with a field of cattle opposite the widely-spaced houses. Constable Lyntley approached the first door which, I noticed, was in need of a coat of paint, and beat upon it with his fist.

"Charlie, come out! The sergeant wants to see you."

For some moments there was silence, save for the lowing of the cattle, then the door was flung open to reveal a white-faced young man in a collarless shirt.

"Tell him I'm not well. I'll be in tomorrow."

"Sick, you say?" retorted his colleague. "Too much ale, more like. You always were one for the bottle, it'll be the end of you."

"You know that, and I know that," Constable Martin agreed, "but Sergeant Redfern doesn't. Let it stay like that."

He was about to close the door, but then seemed to be aware of the presence of Holmes and myself for the first time. He made to speak again, but my friend was quicker.

"There is more to it than that, Constable."

"And who might you be, sir?"

"My name is Sherlock Holmes, and this is my associate, Doctor John Watson."

A tinge of colour suffused his face. "The unofficial detective, from London? I have heard of you. What can you be wanting with me?"

"Perhaps as little as a few words of explanation. I should mention that I am here with the approval of Scotland Yard."

Constable Martin took on a guilty look that he tried to conceal with a sheepish smile. "Ask your questions, then."

"Very well." Holmes gave him a piercing look, but spoke quietly. "What can you tell us about the abduction of the young daughter of a Member of Parliament, Miss Julia Cranmore, who was abducted from her school, Our Lady of Divine Grace. We have reason to believe that she is being held within this area, and that there is a connection with a German spy ring."

"I know nothing of any of this," he stammered.

"Your expression suggests otherwise. As an officer of the law, can there be any reason why you would object to a search of these premises?"

"You'd better let us in, Charlie," said Constable Lyntley.

We were admitted to a rather drab room, with our host now in an obvious state of distress. He wrung his hands, and panic was written on his face.

"They forced me, you see," he blurted out suddenly. "I have relations in Germany, on my dear mother's side, and they said they would visit them in the night, to kill them."

"Who made these threats?" Holmes asked.

"Two men came, they gave no names. They described my cousins and where they live and a lot more things, and said that they would be safe if I did as I was told."

"And what were their orders?"

"To keep Miss Cranmore hidden."

"Did these men mention the name 'Veidermann'?

"Not at all."

"Yet you were heard to mention it, at your place of employment. How did you come to know of it?"

There was a moment of silence, during which Constable Martin's fearful expression was partially replaced by bewilderment. I sensed that something had changed here.

"I remember now," he began, giving his colleague a confused look, "it was in the telegram from London."

"Which I intercepted and clumsily dropped. You retrieved it for me, reading part of the message." We all turned to Constable Lyntley. "If my superiors in Berlin found out, they would certainly disapprove most strongly of my carelessness."

I glanced at Holmes, who did not appear surprised. Indeed, a faint smile of satisfaction dominated his expression. He noted, almost casually, the revolver in Constable Lyntley's hand.

"You, I have no doubt, were in charge of this end of the spy ring's operation," my friend said to him. "Your function would have been to provide the threat to Mr Cranmore that ensured his assistance in gaining information about the parade where our Queen was to be assassinated."

"Much more than that, Mr Holmes. I was installed here like many others, throughout your miserable country, some time ago. We knew, my comrades and I, that the real Lyntley was due to arrive here to take up his duties, and it fell to me to intercept and dispose of him before assuming his identity. I believe that the body was never discovered. Acting on recent instructions, I arranged for some of my associates to abduct the girl and bring her here in secret. Martin was our unwitting accomplice, completely unaware that one of his colleagues was controlling his life. In fact, both of those blundering fools who I work with at the station have never suspected my purpose, nor who I truly am. They has been long in preparation, but we have planned devastating blows to your royal family, and then your government, until you are ripe for invasion."

Holmes shrugged. "But the plot was discovered."

"On this occasion. There will be others that succeed."

"And now?"

"I had intended to come here soon, in any case. It is essential to our plans to silence both the girl and Martin," he looked at his colleague expressionlessly, "for the sake of our future security. Now, it appears, I will have to dispose of you and your companion similarly. I will arrange things so that Martin is blamed. I do not think that Sergeant Redfern will be difficult to convince and, after all, Martin will be unable to deny his guilt."

Holmes turned to me. "Well, Watson, we seem to be in a desperate situation. I find it rather reminiscent of that Nigel Melhuish business of a few months ago."

I knew then what I had to do. My friend had left our escape, our survival, to me. The Melhuish affair had ended in an unrehearsed and effective way, and Holmes' hidden instruction was to act now as I had then. I was not, therefore, surprised by his next words.

"You appear to have the upper hand, Constable Lyntley, or whatever your true name may be." He raised his hands in surrender and walked across the room to stand beside the astounded Constable Martin. In doing so he passed between our adversary and myself for no more than a fleeting moment, but it was enough for me to draw my service weapon. Also to our advantage was that Lyntley was watching Holmes, still following his movement at the instant that I fired. The report echoed dully around the small room and the smell of cordite filled the air. Lyntley had let his weapon fall to the floor, from a hand now shattered and dripping with blood. Through his agony, he cursed us in his native language.

"It seems that things have turned out quite satisfactorily, despite everything," said Holmes. "Well done, Watson. Do what you can for him, old fellow, the hangman must not be disappointed." He retrieved Lyntley's revolver and put it into his pocket, before turning to Constable Martin. "I cannot say what lies in the future for you, but I will ensure that it is understood that you were forced to act as you did."

The constable murmured something that could have been thanks, and I saw that the unexpected events had produced severe shock in him. I bound Lyntley's arm as best that I could in the absence of my medical bag, with two of his own large handkerchiefs. He groaned continually, as his unaffected arm was handcuffed to a stout oak table, but neither Holmes or myself felt sympathy. We left Constable Martin on guard with Lyntley's gun and instructions to fire at the slightest threat as we climbed the creaking stairs to an attic room. Using the key we had been given we entered to find a pretty auburn-haired girl sitting morosely in a chair. She appeared to have been treated well, there was food and water and, although relieved to see us, she was less distressed than I expected. When I had determined that she was ready to leave we descended, and I noted her fearful response to the sight of Lyntley and, to a lesser degree, of Martin. The constable was able to borrow a cart from the neighbouring farm, and we set off for the station soon after.

"It would seem that we have left Sergeant Redfern with something of a problem," Holmes observed as our train gathered speed the following morning. "However, the loss of both his constables will doubtlessly be corrected by replacements from Norwich, before long."

We leaned back in our seats, smoking peacefully.

"Holmes," I said presently, "Yesterday, at Constable Martin's house, I had the distinct impression that you were already aware of Lyntley's true identity before he revealed himself."

He nodded. "It is true that I suspected that he was not all that he seemed. My conclusions were based on his pronunciation – although faint, his German accent was discernible to me at times, and his familiarity with German names. Who would have thought that a village constable would know that 'Martin' was a name common to this country as well as Germany?" He smiled and peered from the window, before emptying his pipe into the ash-tray. "Watson, I would prefer you not to include this case in your over-romanticised accounts to your publisher."

I looked at him, curiously. "Why ever not? You concluded it successfully."

"I consider it a partial success only, since the last act was founded, at first, on an erroneous premise."

"How so? I confess to being confused."

"At the time we arrived at Constable Martin's home, my supposition was quite wrong. I had thought that Martin and Lyntley were both our adversaries, and it was only when I observed the effect of our presence on Martin that the truth became apparent to me. A hardened German agent would not have responded to exposure like that."

"I imagine that Lyntley will encounter Mycroft's people, before long."

"They will question him, it is certain. Let us hope that they will learn something to our country's advantage, before he meets the hangman."

I took out my pocket-watch. "We should be back at Baker Street within the hour. Have you much awaiting your attention?"

"Nothing urgent, as I recall. There is of course the post which has accumulated in our absence, but I am not of a mind to deal with that immediately. What do you say, old fellow, to an afternoon at St James Hall? After the luncheon which Mrs Hudson has doubtlessly prepared for us, a violin recital of some skill would be soothing to the nerves."

Also from Arthur Hall

In addition to the six books in the Rediscovered Cases series, Arthur is a regular contributor to the MX Book of New Sherlock Holmes Stories – the world's largest collection of traditional short stories.

Arthur has released two collections of those same stories as separate books.

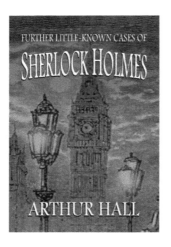 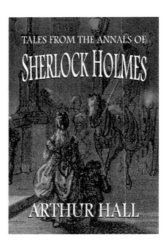

Further Little Known Cases of Sherlock Holmes and Tales From The Annals of Sherlock Holmes. You can see all Arthur's books on his profile page:

https://mxpublishing.com/collections/sherlockian-author-profile-arthur-hall

Also from MX Publishing

MX Publishing is the world's largest specialist Sherlock Holmes publisher, with over a hundred titles and fifty authors creating the latest in Sherlock Holmes fiction and non-fiction.

From traditional short stories and novels to travel guides and quiz books, MX Publishing cater for all Holmes fans.

The collection includes leading titles such as *Benedict Cumberbatch In Transition* and *The Norwood Author* which won the 2011 Howlett Award (Sherlock Holmes Book of the Year).

MX Publishing also has one of the largest communities of Holmes fans on Facebook with regular contributions from dozens of authors.

https://www.facebook.com/BooksSherlockHolmes

www.mxpublishing.com

Also From MX Publishing

Traditional Canonical Holmes Adventures by
David Marcum

Creator and editor of
The MX Book of New Sherlock Holmes Stories

 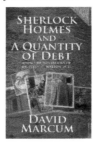 

The Papers of Sherlock Holmes

"The Papers of Sherlock Holmes *by David Marcum contains nine
intriguing mysteries . . . very much in the classic tradition . . . He writes
well, too.*" – Roger Johnson, Editor, *The Sherlock Holmes Journal*,
The Sherlock Holmes Society of London

"Marcum offers nine clever pastiches."
– Steven Rothman, Editor, *The Baker Street Journal*

Sherlock Holmes and A Quantity of Debt

"*This is a welcome addendum to Sherlock lore that respectfully fleshes
out
Doyle's legendary crime-solving couple in the context of new escapades
. . . .*" – Peter Roche, Examiner.com

"*David Marcum is known to Sherlockians as the author of two short story
collections . . . In* Sherlock Holmes and A Quantity of Debt, *he
demonstrates mastery of the longer form as well.*"
– Dan Andriacco, Sherlockian and Author of the Cody and McCabe Series

Sherlock Holmes – Tangled Skeins

(Included in Randall Stock's, 2015 Top Five Sherlock Holmes Books – Fiction)
"*Marcum's collection will appeal to those who like the traditional
elements of the Holmes tales.*" – Randall Stock, BSI

"*There are good pastiche writers, there are great ones, and then
there is David Marcum who ranks among the very best . . .
I cannot recommend this book enough.*"
– Derrick Belanger, Author and Publisher of Belanger Books

Also from MX Publishing

 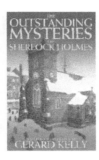 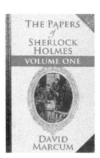

Our bestselling books are our short story collections;

'Lost Stories of Sherlock Holmes' , 'The Outstanding Mysteries of Sherlock Holmes', The Papers of Sherlock Holmes Volume 1 and 2, 'Untold Adventures of Sherlock Holmes' (and the sequel 'Studies in Legacy) and 'Sherlock Holmes in Pursuit', 'The Cotswold Werewolf and Other Stories of Sherlock Holmes' – and many more......

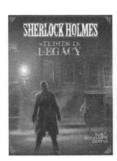  

www.mxpublishing.com

Also from MX Publishing

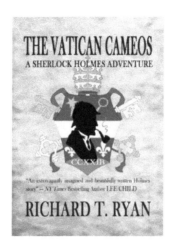

When the papal apartments are burgled in 1901, Sherlock Holmes is summoned to Rome by Pope Leo XII. After learning from the pontiff that several priceless cameos that could prove compromising to the church, and perhaps determine the future of the newly unified Italy, have been stolen, Holmes is asked to recover them. In a parallel story, Michelangelo, the toast of Rome in 1501 after the unveiling of his Pieta, is commissioned by Pope Alexander VI, the last of the Borgia pontiffs, with creating the cameos that will bedevil Holmes and the papacy four centuries later. For fans of Conan Doyle's immortal detective, the game is always afoot. However, the great detective has never encountered an adversary quite like the one with whom he crosses swords in "The Vatican Cameos.."

"An extravagantly imagined and beautifully written Holmes story"
(**Lee Child**, NY Times Bestselling author, Jack Reacher series)

Lightning Source UK Ltd.
Milton Keynes UK
UKHW020939080622
404120UK00009B/618